www.therealcreativevizions.com

TRENCH TALK:

A Chiraq Hood Tale

UN1QUE SALAAM

This book is a work of fiction. Names, characters, places, and incidents either are products of the author's imagination or are used fictitiously. Any resemblances to actual events or locals or persons, living or dead, is entirely coincidental.

Copyright © 2024 by Un1que Salaam

All rights reserved, including rights to reproduce this book or portions thereof in any form whatsoever.

Manufactured in the United States of America

DEDICATION

This book is dedicated to all my loved ones that returned to Allah before this project was completed or even thought about: Uncle Sam; Lulu; Big Chucky (Wild Wild); Larry (I miss you like a mug bro); Nana (love you with all of me); Ma (I enjoyed every second with you, even up to your last days, and I'm thankful I got to spend that time with you); Big Peter (thank you for being there for our family, you're missed); Jackie (I love & miss you); Mac Mont & Young Lawless (I love y'all to the core & I'ma go hard for y'all); Man Man (if only you knew my heart and how your untimely departure impacted us).

I can never forget my first *true* love, Kam, you mean the world to me. Despite all my flaws, shortcomings, and screw ups, I hope that one day you'll see me at my core not for the things I did or what you heard. My love for you has never wavered, and no woman has been able to fill my heart the way you have.

To every Mob, Click, and Hood in Chicago—this for y'all. I *love* the City. We *gotta* do better, we *can* do better, we *shall* do better. Ain't *nothing* fly about all the killing, especially those innocent civilians. *Wake up*!!!!! The *game* is just that, a *game*. You betting against the house, it's *not* designed for us to win, it's designed for the *house* to win *every* time. The small victories we celebrate through killing ain't really victory, it's a loss *all* the way around. You got your man, but you killed his family too; you killed your family when that lick back come or when the slave catchers arrest you and put you on the plantation. *We* have the power to change the City, change the culture--use your voice. You either part of the problem or part of the solution, use your mind, look at the bigger picture. Play chess not checkers!!!

To all the troubled youth worldwide there's better ways to move. The graveyard and jail *ain't* it. You hold the power of your future and the world on top of your shoulders and in the palm of your hands, use it beneficially. No matter your situation, there's someone that loves you and wanna see you succeed, count me amongst whoever that may be for you!

THANKS

I thank Allah ta'ala for granting me the ability to express myself with words and giving me a creative mind to share with the world, and for using me as a vessel to positively impact anyone that He decreed by their interaction with me or my books. I ask that abundant prayers and blessings be bestowed upon His servant and Messenger, Prophet Muhammad (ﷺ) until the Day of Judgment.

Thank you to everyone that genuinely supported me, believed in me, and willingly loved me before, during and after this process. I truly appreciate each and every one of you, you know who you are. J-Mula (State to the Lake) I appreciate your input, criticism, and ideas Gang; and I hope this will inspire you to move different, move better--ain't *nun* behind them walls.

P. Wise thank you for your incredible artwork, you're amazing in your ability to manifest what I envisioned. I appreciate you.

TRENCH TALK:

A Chiraq Hood Tale

1

<u>Sunday, September 3, 2023</u>

It was 2 a.m. when 16-year-old Malik Williams, 'Man', as he was nicknamed by his mother, was awakened in a startled state by loud noises breaking his peaceful rest. Five loud gun shots rang out that could be felt through the brick walls of a Chicago house, Boom, boom, boom, boom, boom. Man had grown accustomed to hearing random shots, but this time it was different. They were closer, louder, and penetrating; the shots seemed to have shaken his house. He felt the echo of each shot throughout his body.

Man was paralyzed with fear as he laid stiff in utter shock with his body magnetized to his bed. In captivating terror, the thought dawned on him that maybe *he'd* been shot. He had become Chicago's next 'vic'. In a panic, he anxiously wanted to search his body for wetness or holes. However, he was unsure if an intruder was in his house or not. Details of what happened were still registering in his semi-groggy mind, so he didn't move. It seemed like an eternity that he'd been lying there playing possum, although it'd only been seconds, literally.

Man couldn't resist another second. He *needed* to know if he'd been shot, whether intentionally or accidentally. He wasn't ready to die; he was afraid, and the more he thought about it, the more he panicked. Finally, his hands scoured his flat chest and torso. Discovering everything intact, he felt a sense of relief. *Wait!* he thought. *My legs, I need'em.* Quickly, he curled his shins to the side as his hands slid over every portion of his legs from the thighs to his feet. He sighed. "Good lookin', God."

As he was getting out of bed to close and lock the raggedy window in his room, which he always left cracked open at night, he heard footsteps. Man paused, hesitated, trying to make sense of it. The footsteps became louder and were closing in on him. "Damn!" he exclaimed softly as he put his back flat against the wall to the right of the window and watched a shadow zip past his bedroom window, then disappear in an instant. He reached to his right and grabbed the Easton aluminum baseball bat from his Jackie Robinson league days. Man clutched the bat tightly and inched towards the window, cautiously peeking out, slightly holding the curtain. After assuring the coast was clear, Man removed the half of the pencil he kept wedged in the window frame's track and closed the metal latch lock at the top.

Still unclear of what exactly transpired, Man inched his way to his mother Diamond's room in the back of the house to check on her. It was total darkness, but he knew his way around. He switched the bat to his left hand to use his right hand to follow the wall to her room. Upon arriving at Diamond's room, he called out in a low voice, "Mama, you up? You, okay?"

Diamond stood to the left of her bedroom window, peeking out into her backyard that was adjacent to the alley while holding her Glock 19 firmly pointed at the floor looking like the female version of Malcolm X. "I'm good baby, stay right there for a second and be quiet," she whispered. Diamond scanned the backyard and alley for any more activity. She was ready to shoot first and call 911 later.

Her assurance was gained after a few minutes of nothingness, then the silence was broken by the clicking of Diamond turning on the lamp resting on her nightstand.

She sat on the side of her king-sized bed and looked at Man standing in *awe* with his bat like he was at the plate. "Boy, what's wrong with you, looking like you saw a ghost. I should be asking if you okay, shoot."

Man stumbled with his words. "Mama, what the heck you doin' wit' a pipe? Where you get that from?"

Diamond chuckled as she put her Glock 19 back in its case and locked it. "What I'm doing with a *what?* Man, we live on the south side of Chicago, boy. I been here my entire life, you think I don't know how to survive or protect my son? Don't no man live here, we on our own, why you think I gave you your nickname?"

Tension easing, Man walked into his mother's room.

"And don't worry about where I got my gun from. I may go to work and take care of you, but I also know how to hold my own. All you need to know is I'm legit and 'ain't for nun' as y'all like to say," Diamond further stated sliding the gun case back under her bed.

Man, hesitantly pressed his mom. "I'm just confused mama, all my life you taught me to stay away from guns, yet you own one, you contradicting yourself. "

"No, I'm not contradicting myself. Yes, I taught you to stay away from guns so that you don't wind up like these fools shooting through all of Chicago, killing people. So that you won't end up locked up in IYC or Cook County jail and because you don't have no gun training. I have gun training; I'm licensed, and most importantly, I'm grown."

Diamond went to her son, gently grabbed his face, and held his cheeks. "*That's* the difference between you and me, Man. And what's that word you used, where you get that from? Didn't I tell you to stay from them thugs, so you don't wind up like this fool shooting behind our house? Man, stay on the path you're on and make a life for yourself, son. You don't have to stay in the 100s all of your life."

"Mama, I know. I don't be with them like that, but that don't mean ion hear or know the slang, rules, etc. I told you when I go pro, I'm gonna buy you a house and get you outta Chicago. You and grandma and grandpa."

Diamond smiled. "I know baby, but don't worry about us, we're gonna be okay. We just want to make sure you don't become a Chicago statistic. Go back to bed and get your rest. You got school tomorrow." She kissed Man on the cheek. "Goodnight, I love you." She told him.

<u>Monday, September 4, 2023</u>

A few hours later, Man was awakened to get up for school. He got up and turned on his music, plugged in the iron, grabbed the ironing board and stretched it out, then went into the bathroom to brush his teeth and wash his face. When he finished in the bathroom, Man went to his closet to pick an outfit for the day. He decided on a pair of True Religion jeans and a matching hoodie, which he then ironed, creased, and starched like a real Chicagoan. After ironing his outfit, Man laid it across his bed, then went and hopped in the shower.

While Man was getting ready, Diamond cooked breakfast. Some scrambled eggs with cheese and hash browns–his favorite. Diamond poured Man a glass of chilled, pure orange juice and called him to eat.

After getting Man settled, Diamond opened her kitchen window and lit a Kool cigarette, then blew a mouthful of smoke outside, holding the cigarette in the air, like she was a woman at the Kentucky Derby smoking a cigarette from a cigarette tip. For a split second, Diamond slipped into a trance, then quickly snapped out of it. "How'd you sleep?" she asked Man.

Man paused his drinking to answer. "Aight, I guess. Mama, when you gone quit smoking?"

"When I don't have no more worries, Man," Diamond retorts, looking over her shoulder at him.

"When's that gonna be?"

"Baby," Diamond softly said. "When I can get us outta this jungle and get a better job, all my problems will be solved. Finish eating so we can go."

Diamond finished her cigarette just as Man finished up his breakfast.

"I'll clean up. You get your things and let's get out of here," Diamond said.

Man returned to his room, and grabbed his book-bag, and wind-breaker. He took everything into the living room and sat it all on the floor then stood in the body-length mirror hanging on the wall and stared into the mirror, double-checking everything about his attire from the hoodie to his Jordans. Last, Man straightened his eyebrows with his thumb and index finger to complete his look to perfection.

Diamond stood spying on her son in admiration but busted out in complete laughter when he fixed his eyebrows. "Get yo arrogant ass out the mirror boy and come on. Them little girls ain't thinking about you."

"Hating is a weakness, Mama. Use that salt to season your food, not hate on me."

They laughed together, then got into Diamond's car so that she could drop him off at Percy L. Julian High School, and then head to work. She was a shift manager at Jewels', a grocery store chain.

2

Diamond and Man had been through a lot, individually and collectively. Some things were by choice, while others were pure circumstance. Although they lived in one of the tough neighborhoods in Chicago, the Wild 100s, neither of them had succumbed completely to their environment.

Diamond was raised by both of her parents in the same neighborhood she and her son were living in. Her father, Horace, was now an honorably discharged military veteran and her mother, Carrie, was on the brink of retiring from her insurance selling career. Good morals and values were instilled in Diamond throughout her life. She attended church every Sunday with her parents at Unity Baptist. Diamond maintained a GPA of 3.5 or higher throughout her tenure as a student.

Despite her parents doing everything in their power to set her on the right path, they couldn't completely shield her from the bowels of the hood. As a 170 pound, 5'8" redbone with permed, silky, brown hair that rested mid-back. Her slim-thick physique was accompanied by natural beauty and intelligence that exceeded most of her peers. Diamond naturally attracted boys.

Throughout high school, Diamond kept a boyfriend or two, but nobody she took seriously because she knew they'd only wanted to get between her long, athletic-styled legs. Her beauty and intelligence also got her in trouble with her female peers. Diamond found herself getting into unnecessary fights. Girls thought she was stuck up, or that she was trying to steal their boyfriends.

Diamond was raised to be non-judgmental, so she often gave the wrong guy a chance. After she graduated high school, she enrolled at Chicago State University to pursue a Bachlor's degree in Nursing.

As she was walking off campus to her 2006 Honda Accord, a guy approached her in his 2007 Mercedes Benz Brabus S550. He had a sharp fade, stood 6'6" and weighed a solid 215 pounds, without an ounce of fat on him because he was in the gym at least three times a week. He had a caramel complexion and an easy-going swagger about himself.

The Brabus slowed down as Note locked eyes with Diamond. She bashfully dropped her head. Note, as he was better known, stopped the car, and dimmed his music. "How's the beautiful lady doing today?" he asked smoothly.

Diamond looked around then behind her, intimating he wasn't addressing her. There was no one else around.

"Who you talking to?"

"You're the only one around that's caught my eye."

Diamond blushed harder. "Well, in that case, I'm fine. And you?"

"I asked how you're doing, gorgeous, not how you lookin'."

Diamond smiled wide and let out a slight chuckle. "Thank you. I'm well."

"You'll be even better with me in your life. You gotta man?"

She slightly twisted her face in disbelief at his cap yet left the door open for Note. "Ain't nothing but boys around here, so no, ion have a man."

Note released a light laugh before replying, "I'm sorry you feel that way, but how about you take my card and call me sometime? Gimme the opportunity to prove you wrong. "

Diamond accepted the card and read it. She extended her hand. "I'm Diamond. Pleased to meet you. I'll think about calling you, Mr. Smooth."

"Diamond, huh? The name is fitting, you certainly been carved out right from my vantage point," Note said, checking out her body. "I'm Note and the pleasure's all mine. Don't think too long or hard. I'll be waiting for you."

Man would result from Diamond and Note. Although Diamond had become a single mother, having her parents as her support system helped. To the best of her ability, Diamond instilled in Man the same and more values her parents had instilled in her.

Since that warm summer day in 2007 when she met Note, Diamond couldn't stop thinking about him or shake the butterflies she had in her stomach. A week had passed, and Diamond had done no more than read his business card and twirl it around in her hand while contemplating whether to call him. Of course, he was good looking, had a decent physique from what she could tell, a gentleman's manners, and a beyond-luxury Benz. He had a seemingly 'ain't for none' demeanor, yet he knew how to handle it pretty well.

He was the complete package, but one strike he apparently had against him from her perspective… he was likely in the game. Meaning he sold drugs, burglarized houses, or probably committed fraud. Regardless, it was something that would ultimately land him in prison one day, and she wasn't cut out for that lifestyle.

Granted, the business card reveals he's the owner of a freight company. But he was young driving the latest Benz, a brand she had to Google to learn more about it. Certainly, his business couldn't be *that* successful. *This the caliber of guy that my parents been warning me about,* thought

Diamond. *I gotta sleep on this one a little more.* She could hear her mom's voice. "Baby, when something seems too good to be true, it usually is." Slowly, Diamond drifted away in a trance until she drifted off thinking about Note.

Over the next few days, Diamond would perform her daily activities: running errands; helping Carrie keep house; applying for jobs; and striving to enjoy the beautiful Chicago weather without becoming its next innocent victim of gang violence.

While everyone else who graduated from Julian High School was primarily enjoying their summer turning up, Diamond was adamant about finding a job to stack some money and get her own spot to enable her to experience and feel some form of independence. After all, she was an adult now and therefore wanted to start her journey to getting on her grown woman stuff.

As Diamond carried on with her days, she still thought about Note. It had been nearly two weeks. Even when she wasn't thinking about him, she would see a gray car, triggering her thoughts to the Benz with the black interior and chrome wheels, or a gym commercial would pop up on TV, reminding her of his muscular frame.

Diamond's gut faintly warned her to not get involved with Note, yet her mind urged her to go for it. She could care less how much money he had or about the car he drove because she was far from a gold-digger. It was his vibe… almost like he had put a spell on her telepathically. He said all the right things, at the right moments and exhibited an aura of confidence that wasn't flamboyant.

Friday, June 22, 2007

Two weeks later, Note finally heard the alert on his phone that he'd been hoping for. He checked the messages.

"Hey"

He was clueless about who was texting him. It was a number he didn't recognize. So he responded hesitantly, asking who it was. He knew from the verbiage that it was a female, just uncertain which one. Note sat and thought momentarily. He sent another text with the diamond emoji, hoping that who was contacting him.

Upon seeing the emoji, Diamond smiled and sent Note heart eyes for confirmation. How did he know it was her? Maybe he wasn't that bad after all. When Note texted back for her to call him because he was driving, Diamond gasped. But still encouraged herself to hit the call button.

"Hey beautiful, how are you?" He answered.

"I'm fine. How are you?"

"I'm blessed, sweetheart. Thank you for asking. So, I got you blushing already and it ain't even been three minutes yet?"

Diamond chuckled in embarrassment. Note detected something he hadn't visually seen. "A little. Your charm comes off so naturally, I take it you make countless women blush."

"I wouldn't say all that, but I'm good for a smile or two."

"Only one or two?"

"How about we let you be the judge?" Note shot back smoothly.

Diamond pictured him leaning against his driver's door, gripping the top of his steering wheel like a man in complete control of everything in his life.

"I like the sound of that Note," Diamond said softly. "How'd you know it was me texting you? Was it a lucky guess?"

"Nah, it wasn't a lucky guess at all. Contrary to popular belief, I don't give my card to many women. The select few who have my line are already saved, so I was pretty sure it was you."

"Ahhhh, ok, so you low-key cheated?" Diamond chuckled.

"Listen, it's nice outside today. If you're not busy, can I come pick you up for lunch and we can use that time getting acquainted?"

Diamond wasted no time accepting Note's offer. "You know, I'd be pleased to have lunch with you while we relate and exchange. Can you give me about an hour to get myself together?"

"For sure, that's perfect. I'm in the middle of an errand, so I'll head your way when I'm done. Text me your address and closest cross streets so I know where I'm going. I'll send you a text when I'm in your area."

"Okay, thank you. I'll send you my address now. See you shortly."

"God willing, we'll see each other in an hour."

After finishing his call with Diamond, Note called his receptionist, Marilyn, at his warehouse, United Front Freight, and had her make last minute reservations at The Island's Wellness Spa for Diamond. He drove home to shower, change clothes, and strap on his Glock 40. Instead of just having lunch, he had planned to spend the rest of the day with Diamond. He was unsure when they'd be able to spend time together again given his often-busy schedule, but he had time today.

Upon leaving his crib, Note jumped back in the Brabus and pulled out his Midland GXT1000VP4 2-way radio to reach his right-hand man, Jerome, or J-Boogie as he was known. "Yo, Boogie what's da word G?"

"At the Trap, what's the deal?"

"Sit tight, I'm through there."

"Say less. Love."

"Love."

Within 15 minutes, Note was pulling into the UFF parking lot, where he parked next to J-Boogie's 745 BMW. He climbed the few stairs leading into his company's office where he was greeted by his receptionist, Marilyn.

Marilyn had been long itching to get her run with Note. He was privy to Marilyn's lustful desires and he Heisman-trophied her every effort because he also knew she just wanted to eat off of his fortune. Eat more that is. Note was already paying her a $65k salary with medical, dental, and optical benefits. Regardless of how fine, thick, hardworking, and loyal Marilyn was, her ulterior motives disinterested him in any intimate involvement with her. He was smart enough to know that sex or any other intimacy with her would only complicate things for him and his business, so he intentionally kept it professional and cordial.

As he entered UFF's lobby, Note saw J-Boogie in the warehouse talking to an employee. "J", Note called out.

When J-Boogie saw Note, they headed to Note's private office and sat in their respective seats.

"What's da deal, bro?" asked J-Boogie.

"I need you to hold it down for the rest of the day, and possibly night. Shordy I told you about not too long ago tapped in today and I'm bouta snatch her up for lunch, but she don't know I plan to have her the rest of the day, ya dig? Next couple weeks gonna be chaos for us, so I gotta get up wit her now."

"Bet. You know I got you. It's not too busy today, so I'm here pretty much all day, and I'll have Marilyn forward all your calls to me. You tryna hit ol' girl already tho?"

Naw, I ain't on that, Gang. The vibes with her is different, so I wanna spend some time with her and see if it's really a vibe or a façade she got going on. When I take her back home, I'll know what I needta. I see potential in her, but I needta know if she sees the same or if it can even move on the level of her potential. Time is money, ion like wasting either."

"Facts!" they both declared.

J-Boogie wasn't surprised Note wanted to talk in person, that was his preference; discuss all business in private without the government or opps being able to tune in.

Note spent an arm and a leg soundproofing and installing counter-surveillance equipment in his office and vehicles once he got plugged with the Colombian cartel. Despite only being 21 years old, Note was sharp. He had grown up fast and was laced by his parents from an early age. Anything pertaining to plays or his personal moves were discussed in his secure office, in person, or over his private and modified 2-way radios.

3

Note left his short meeting with J-Boogie and hopped back in the Brabus to pick up Diamond. He sent her a text message: "You about ready"?

Diamond: "Yes."

"I'm on my way, be there in 20."

Note jumped on the Dan Ryan expressway, heading to the south side. He merged into the fast lane, quickly got the Brabus to 70 mph, and turned on his Fat Money playlist to cruise to. Note reached his 95th Street exit in no time and took the off-ramp to head into the trenches—the Wild 100s. Note took Halsted Street to 105th Street then to S. Sangamon. He made a left as he inched his way down the block, paying attention to the addresses.

Elders were sitting in chairs on their porches enjoying the weather and watching over the children playing on the block who were enjoying the water shooting out the opened fire hydrant. A raggedy ice cream truck was trailing him down Sangamon with its music blaring over the PA system. When Note neared the pouring fire hydrant, all the children disbursed to the sides of the street.

Note pulled up on about 8 children of different ages. He rolled down the driver's side window and called out. "Aye, y'all know where Diamond live?"

"We 'on know nothin'! You ain't from round here, you might be a opp!" one kid pressed.

Note laughed and entertained the youngster. "Do yo opps come through here in a Benz riding solo and dressed like me, shordy?"

"Man, it's 2007, da opps come through in all kinds of steamers, whatchu talmbout?" The boy shot back with aggression.

Note could do nothing more than shake his head, roll up his window, and drive past the water that one of the older children had thankfully turned down for the vehicles to pass. All the while, Note thought, *lil bad ass kid*. He grabbed his phone and texted Diamond: "I'm here, pop out."

He continued inching down the block until he spotted her address. Diamond was simultaneously stepping out of her parents' house. Note pulled over to let the ice cream truck pass and Diamond made her way to the Brabus and got in. She exchanged greetings with Note before he went back to Halsted, made a left and headed towards the Dan Ryan expressway and took the 95th Street on-ramp.

Diamond was astonished at how comfortable and engulfing the Brabus cabin was. She quickly and easily felt completely immersed in luxury, as she scoped out the Brabus' interior and extravagant technology.

After some short-lived small talk, Diamond asked, "So what you got planned, Note?"

"Honestly, after further thought, I was hoping to get the rest of today with you. My plans are contingent upon whether you're gonna let me show you what I desire. Whatchu think about that?"

"What is it that you desire?"

"I wanna show you a good time, some things you've probably never experienced, nothing bogish."

"Aw, ok. I'm open to spending the day with you, I don't really have no plans today, so I got time."

"That's what's up. You won't be disappointed, trust me."

Note went to downtown Chicago and parked his car in a secured parking garage. The two of them then walked over to the beach and began walking along the Lakefront Trail while engaging in conversation.

Diamond, an introvert, could often be bashful, but more often, she's known for being a straight shooter. "So let's start with your name." She dove right in, questioning him.

"What about my name, whatchu wanna know?"

"For starters, how about your real name? Then you can explain the C-Note thing."

"Aight. So, my government name is Sean Johnson, and C-Note is actually an acronym for Chicago Nigga On Top of Everything. My mom gave me the nickname when I was younger and it stuck with me my whole life. I foolishly changed it to the acronym. As I began maturing, I dropped the acronym and just stuck with 'Note' to keep life simple."

"Wow, that's interesting. I can see your perspective."

"What about you, Diamond your government?" He returned the question.

"Of course, it's my real name. I'm a lady, ion rock no handles. My mom wanted me to have that name to remind my daddy secretly that she wanted a reasonable sized diamond when they got their money right."

"I see. You women have some cold, underhanded ways, straight up."

"I know, right! Well, at least it worked. She eventually got what she wanted. My daddy wound up spending 10 bands on her wedding ring about 17 years ago."

"Whoa! So, your parents been married for 17 years?" Note asked in complete awe.

"Yeah, they married almost a year before I was born."

"That's *heavy*! You don't really see that kind of longevity in da Black community, ya know? Especially in

Chicago. That kinda commitment is hard to maintain. That's a true manifestation of loyalty and dedication. Speaking of which, what's your take on loyalty?"

"Whatchu mean, can you be more specific?"

"What I'm asking is how do you feel about loyalty? Is it something you implement in your life?"

"Aw, ok. Well, I'm from Chicago, and ya know our ideology. If you don't have loyalty, you ain't real. My mom always taught me about loyalty and extending it to those who deserve it rather than any and everybody. So, it's not something I give freely anymore. I've learned from my mistakes in doing that. But I give it where it's earned or deserved."

"I can definitely relate to that. You've learned some valuable life lessons to be as young as you are. A wise man once said, *'When people show loyalty to you, you take care of those who are with you. It's how it goes with everything. If you have a small circle of friends and one of those friends doesn't stay loyal to you, they don't stay your friend for very long.'* I live by that kinda perspective."

"Thank you, but you act like you *way* older than me or sumn'," Diamond said, bursting into laughter. "You didn't say anything about exercising. Is this your plan, to spend Lord knows how much time walking and talking?"

"Nah, I wanna give you a *taste* of Chicago." Note said slyly.

"The Taste don't start until next month, whatchu mean?"

"I didn't say *The* Taste of Chicago, I said *a* taste of Chicago. I don't attend any functions where my life is likely or even possibly at risk, so I haven't been to da Taste since I was a shordy. "

The couple made their way back to the car after about an hour of getting acquainted, and Note drove to a new location—The Island, a 5-star hotel in downtown Chicago. He parked in front of a set of heavy gold-framed glass doors. A few valet workers were waiting outside for arriving customers.

"Good morning, sir." Note was greeted by a man gently opening his driver's side door for him.

Diamond simultaneously experienced the same on the passenger side. The couple individually exited and Note replied, "Good morning." Eduardo was on the name tag of Note's valet. He was a native Chicagoan Latino born to immigrant Guatemalan parents who fled to the States seeking the American dream. Because of having to speak Spanish to his parents daily, Eddie, as he liked to be called, was buried with a Spanish accent.

"Will you be needing the service of one of our porters today, sir?"

Note handed Eddie a $50 bill from his pants pocket. "No, we're not staying, so make sure you take care of my car."

"Yes sir. Thank you, sir," Eddie said, removing a package he retrieved from his inside vest pocket. He spread a required *The Island* embossed seat cover over the driver's side seat before entering the Benz and driving it into the underground parking garage.

Diamond approached Note, completely astonished as she looked around and took in the immaculate surroundings she never knew existed in her otherwise grave-ridden city. She looked him in his eyes. "Note, this is absolutely beautiful, I'm impressed. *BUT!* None of this, or your money, is gonna get me in a hotel room with you today like I'm one of your buss downs." She said harshly.

Note laughed, then tugged at Diamond's hand. "Shordy chill, I ain't on that. I gotta surprise for you."

They walked towards The Island's entrance doors and were greeted by one of the hotel's concierges, who opened one of the gigantic, heavy brass and glass door for them. Note looked around until he spotted the Receptionist's desk and casually walked in its direction. Diamond, still in complete awe, perused the open floor lobby with all its luxury presentations. She clutched Note's hand tightly and pulled it towards her to get him to stop walking. They stood in one place as Diamond slowly scoured every detail of the lobby. The *Lux Touch* marble flooring and matching 25-foot high columns. The exclusive and eye-catching bronze sculpture by Henry Moore resting under the sunlit atrium in the lobby's center, the exclusive collection of John Boldessari's art accompanying the lobby walls. There was exquisite

European, hand-built furniture. The gargantuan Zenith Charleston chandelier was perfectly placed above the foyer area and embraced the most expensive European pieces. Diamond felt an overwhelming calm that she'd not experienced in her lifetime. In her softest voice, she uttered, "This place is absolutely amazing."

"It's only the beginning, c'mon."

The couple approached the *Lux Touch* marble countertop of the Receptionist's desk and was met by a thick, curvaceous redhead clerk. "Welcome to The Island. My name is Jasmine. Do you all have reservations with us?"

Note politely answered, "Thank you, Jasmine, reservation for 'Diamond."

She hastily typed the name into the keyboard hidden from public view and peered at the monitor sitting behind the keyboard and beneath the countertop. The sole reservation appeared on the colored screen. *Diamond 11 am; Ultimate Indulgence; Wellness Spa; $630 paid by cc.* Jasmine involuntarily felt a sense of jealousy. She couldn't afford such pampering, even with her employee discount. Jasmine tried to remain professional. "Do you know where to go, sir?"

"I do not."

Jasmine looked Note in his eyes with a passion that was clear to Diamond and pointed in the direction behind them to several individual elevator doors, then spoke to Note as if Diamond didn't exist. "Take the elevator to the 19th floor. You can't miss your destination once you get off the elevator."

Note smiled, "Thank you." He reached into his shirt pocket and handed Jasmine a folded $50 bill with his phone number written inside.

4

Note and Diamond made their way to the elevator area and waited for the first one to arrive. Diamond's study of her surroundings was broken by an elevator bell and wide-mouthed double doors opening. The couple stepped into the flawless elevator and Note pushed the dual-purpose button, which displayed the number '19' in numerical characters and braille. Diamond broke the silence by looking up to Note, admiring his 6'6" frame. "That white girl damn near brought *all* the 100s outta me." She informed him with an attitude.

Note glanced down at her. "She wanna be in your shoes. Don't sweat small things then they can never get big."

"I'm not sweating anything, you're not even my man, it's the respect for me. Anyway, you said we're not going to a room, yet we're going to the 19th floor. Note, I'm dead ass serious about what I said when we first got here."

"Cool out, shordy. I'm serious about my reply to what you said earlier."

A bell rang in the elevator and the classical music playing through the elevator speakers paused and an automated computer-generated voice let them know they had arrived at their floor. The elevator slowly halted and the doors smoothly opened. The couple faced an illuminated sign with neon blue writing above two glass doors. It read: *The Island's Wellness Spa.*

Diamond stared at the sign in complete disbelief with her jaw on the ground. She was speechless. Note looked down at her paralyzed face. "You good? Look like you seen a ghost."

"I … I'm … I'm ok." She was practically magnetized to the elevator as she stood, taking in the scene.

Everything was *immaculate. There* wasn't so much as a fingerprint on the glass doors of the Spa's entrance. The gray low pile carpet that paved the hallway and spa lobby looked freshly installed like a shoe had never touched it. "I've never seen *anything* like this, ever. All this luxury is amazing. I can't even lie."

Note grabbed Diamond's hand and chuckled as they stepped out of the elevator. "C'mon, you got an appointment to be at."

"*I* gotta an appointment, not *we* have an appointment?"

"You need it in Chinese or something? I can have Google translate. Yes, *your* appointment. For the next four hours, you'll experience 5-star luxury treatment and have a taste of what it feels like to walk in the shoes of the wealthy. I get the vibe that you're not a materialistic woman, and I dig it, but every woman should get this kinda treatment at least once in a lifetime." Note opened the Spa's entrance door and stepped in after Diamond.

At the front desk, they were met by the receptionist, Aziza. was a 5'3", 140 pounds walking compilation of thick chocolate with a 90s-styled haircut that stayed whipped up, a set of naturally exotic orangish eyes, and enough ass to hold up a pair of baggy jeans while revealing sufficient curvature. She was a Jamaican immigrant with a Chicago attitude, coupled with an alluring sense of professionalism.

"Good morning and welcome to The Island's Wellness Spa. You must be Diamond?" the employee offered as she greeted, then honed in on Diamond.

Surprised, Diamond replied, "I am Diamond, yes."

"Great. I'm Aziza, but you can call me 'Zee'. I'll be your hostess for your reservation. Can I get either of you any refreshments?"

Note and Diamond answered in sync, "No thanks."

Zee continued, "Can you take a few minutes to answer this intake questionnaire please Diamond, so that we can know your allergies, skin type, etc.? I'll collect it when you're done. And then I'll get you processed for treatments. Sir, if you'd like to wait, you can have a seat and enjoy some refreshments and/or movies. You're also at liberty to leave and pick up Diamond later. She'll be done with her treatment at 3 p.m."

"You're in excellent hands. I'll be back around a quarter to 3 to pick you up. Enjoy." Note assured Diamond.

"Okay, thank you so much. I'll see you then." Diamond said, staring at Note.

After processing Diamond's intake questionnaire, Zee advised her that she had a long day ahead of her, so to use the bathroom. She also offered Diamond refreshments.

Diamond politely responded, "I'm fine, thank you."

She followed Zee to the massage room. Zee lightly tapped on the door twice before peeking in and advising the masseuse, "I have your 11 o'clock appointment, Diamond, here."

"Thank you, she can come in," Cheryl kindly stated.

Zee held the door open with her body for Diamond, and after Diamond stepped in, Zee gently closed the door and returned to her desk.

"Good morning, Diamond. How are you?"

"I'm fine, thanks for asking. And yourself?"

"I'm good. Thank you as well. My name is Cheryl and I'll be serving as your masseuse. Have you ever had a full-body massage before?

"No, I haven't."

"Okay, so I'm going to be giving you a 90-minute Swedish massage today. I'm going to step out to have you disrobe and place all of your belongings in this basket which you can then place on the chair there in the corner. Then I'd like for you to lay face down on my table and you can use the folded warm sheet to cover your body." Cheryl then stepped out of the room, leaving Diamond to undress.

Before doing anything, she looked around the spacious and nearly empty massage room, taking in the view. The walls and ceiling were painted a soft beige; a single abstract painting clung to one wall. Cheryl's one-person desk sat catty-cornered from the massage table. In a corner nearest the massage table was a small table that held one Himalayan salt lamp. Both items were shielded by an Oriental partition and directly behind the massage table was a small cart that held various massage oils and other necessities. Diamond stepped back towards the room's entrance, placed her back against the door, and began snapping pictures with her cellphone. She sent them to Note, and then did exactly as Cheryl instructed. Diamond lay on the massage table with her face in the headrest and quickly drifted into a trance from the sounds of nature coming from the speakers of the computer.

A few minutes later, Diamond's peace was broken by two light taps on the door, just as Zee had done earlier. Cheryl cracked the door slightly. "Are you situated, Diamond?" she whispered.

"Yes, I am."

Cheryl entered the room and hung a *Do Not Disturb* sign on the door's external handle before closing it.

"Is the temperature okay for you?" asked Cheryl. "Do you have a music preference?"

"Everything is perfect how you have it."

"Fantastic. If you need a break or have to use the bathroom, just let me know, okay?"

"Okay."

Ninety minutes later, Diamond was awakened by soft taps and an echoed voice. "Diamond …. Diamond." When she came to and opened her eyes toward the feminine voice. Cheryl was standing over her, smiling. Diamond was laying on her back now and covered with a towel rather than lying on her stomach as she last remembered. The fog slowly cleared her mind.

"Your massage is concluded," Cheryl said. " I'm going to step out again while you get dressed. Don't worry about the sheet and towel, you can leave them on the table."

"Oh, wow! I'm so embarrassed. How long was I asleep?" Diamond asked.

Cheryl chuckled. "No need to feel embarrassed My clients fall asleep often." Cheryl stepped out of the room and notified Zee that Diamond was done with her massage.

5

Diamond exited the massage room and found Cheryl waiting against the wall. "Zee is waiting for you upfront to take you to your next treatment. Thank you for your business. Please come again. Here's my card."

Diamond accepted the card and thanked Cheryl, then made her way back to Zee, who was waiting to escort Diamond to her facial appointment. Diamond was handed off to a blonde bombshell named Patsy, who stood 5'3"; 135 pounds; had clear breast implants. She had a loud, Cajun-accented voice. Patsy left Shreveport, Louisiana for Chicago in pursuit of her dream career to be a famous makeup artist, but ultimately changed careers when offered an opportunity to receive free esthetician training and a job with The Wellness Spa.

"Patsy, here's Diamond, your 12:30 appointment."

"Okayyyy, thank you!" Patsy's voice raised. She was smiling hard and poking out her chest. Something she had become accustomed to doing since getting her breast implants. "How ya doing, Ms. Diamond?"

"I'm fine, thank you. Please, call me Diamond. Y'all are making me feel old with all this *Ms.* stuff."

"Yes ma'am, Diamond it is. And I hear you, honey."

Once she sat in Patsy's chair, Diamond again drifted off into another world as Patsy performed her delicate yet precise touches to Diamond's face.

As Patsy took her last steps of Diamond's facial–applying toner, serums, and moisturizers–Diamond woke up from her second nap. Gathering her things, she waited for Zee to pick her up for her next treatment.

Diamond was picked up and handed off to her final treatment—manicure and pedicure. Forty-five minutes would be devoted to her hands and the remaining forty-five minutes would be delicately pampering her feet.

Zee small chatted with Diamond. "You're at the home stretch now, your final treatment. How's your experience been so far?"

"Absolutely mind-blowing. Amazing!" Diamond instantly replied. "I've never experienced anything like this before. I would love to come back, but I can't afford it."

"That's great to hear. But we offer a variety of packages. If the 'Ultimate Indulgence' package is too expensive for your budget, you're welcome to check out some of our more affordable packages with fewer amenities."

The ladies walked into the nail salon and Zee advised Attaya. "Tay, I have your 1:30 appointment here—Diamond."

"Hey Zee, thank you. Hey Diamond, have a seat here."

"You're welcome. Diamond, when you're done with Tay, just meet me back at my desk. Enjoy ladies."

"How are you doing, Diamond?" Attaya asked.

"I'm good, thank you. How are you?"

"*Chile*! Don't get me started cuz I don't wanna spoil your seemingly good day. I'm good though, and thank you as well. According to your reservation, you're paid for the mani and pedi. Any styles or colors that interest you today? There isn't anything I can't do with your nails."

"Nothing fancy. I'll do a French tip for both, thank you."

Attaya began her work and chatted with Diamond to make the job and time go by faster for the both of them.

Note arrived at the Spa at 2:40pm sharp. He wasn't surprised Diamond was still at her appointment. This was a business inside a 5-star hotel, and pampering their clients was necessary. After all, clientele keeps business booming, so it was paramount they leave a lasting impression on their clients.

As Note stepped into the Spa's lobby, Zee promptly addressed him, "Good afternoon, sir. Diamond isn't quite done yet, but she should be wrapping up in the next few minutes. You're welcome to have a seat."

"Good afternoon, and thank you. I'm always punctual for appointments, so no worries, I'll wait."

"Can I get you some refreshments?" asked Zee.

"No thank you, I'm fine."

Note sat down and checked emails on his phone while waiting for Diamond in the lobby.

At 3:05 pm Diamond appeared in the lobby smiling from ear to ear, especially at the sight of Note waiting for her in the Spa's lobby. Unbeknownst to Note, he had won brownie points twice today, not because he was spending money on her or gifting her with surprises, but because he had been timely in picking her up. It was the simple things Diamond had become impressed with. As Diamond matured into her womanhood, she learned through her journey to appreciate and enjoy the simple things in life rather than be materialistic, like most young ladies her age.

When Note and Diamond locked eyes, she smiled even harder. "Heyyyy!" she sang.

Note rose from the comfortable chair, smiling just enough to give her positive vibes before he asked, "How'd they treat you?"

"They treated me so well!" exclaimed Diamond, smiling with an apparent glow.

"Good to hear," Note replied as he handed a folded fifty-dollar bill to Zee to tip for her services.

Zee extended a business card to Diamond. "Thank you for choosing The Island's Wellness Spa. Please come again. Y'all have a great day."

"Bye," they said together, and headed to the elevator.

When Note and Diamond approached the huge brass and glass hotel doors to exit and wait in the valet area, the door was again held open for them by the concierge. Within minutes, Eddie emerged from the underground garage in Note's Brabus, parking directly in front of him and Diamond.

"Thank you for visiting The Island, sir. Please come again," Eddie said, smiling as he exited the vehicle.

"Thank you for your treatment," Note shot back as he got into his car.

Note smoothly inched the luxury car to the Island's exit and waited for traffic to clear on E. Superior Street. Once it did, he applied half of his foot pressure to the gas pedal and skirted out of the hotel's parking lot and took Superior street to N. Michigan Avenue and turned onto the street then took it to E. Oak Street.

Slowly, they approached a tall and narrow building with a pristine inside. Diamond was intrigued. The single parking spot directly in front of Cuyana, a high-end women's clothing store, was vacant. Meanwhile, every surrounding parking spot was occupied by vehicles. She thought it was mere irony that even the parking spaces were seemingly submitting to Note.

Diamond was unaware Note had one of his guys secure the parking spot earlier and left upon receiving a text from Note. His moves were often calculated. He liked his life to be organized and smooth like his character.

This narrow building stood 4 stories tall and was immersed in Chicago's signature--clean red bricks. The windows were crystal clear with just the name Cuyana embroidered atop, allowing anyone to glance in and see its many rows of eloquent clothing on the ground level.

Note removed his keys from the parked car and opened his driver's door. Diamond nervously followed his lead. Once again startled, Diamond looked around in complete amazement, unaware that such beauty, elegance, and serenity existed in Chicago. Note walked around the back of the car. Diamond was waiting on the passenger's side. He grabbed her hand and led her to Cuyana's front doors. Like a gentleman, Note opened the door for his companion and entered behind her. They both deeply inhaled the fresh scent of the new clothes. An unfamiliar yet elegant fragrance lingered through the store.

The couple walked around the first floor until they were politely approached by a store clerk. Note took Diamond through all four floors looking at clothes and having her try on several outfits before choosing a particular one that he found alluring: French Terry belted cropped pants, layered sweatshirt, and matching oversized double loop bag–all cappuccino colored. It rested smoothly against her redbone skin.

While getting checked out, Note saw a pair of Women's Style 8 casual shoes. He looked at the store clerk. "Are those available in a size…" He turned his attention to Diamond, who finished the question. "7."

The clerk went to retrieve the open-toe sandals in Diamond's size.

After making the $1,100 payment, Note pointed back to the dressing rooms, telling Diamond to change into the outfit he just purchased.

Diamond did as she was told and stepped out looking like new money. "Oh, my God! You don't have to do this. I've never been treated like this before. These clothes are *so* comfortable, it feels like I'm wearing nothing, fa real." Diamond carried the Cuyana bag, with her previous outfit folded inside. They made their way out of the store and back to his ride.

Soon they were pulling back up to Lake Michigan. Note parked in a public parking lot, and this time walked nearer the water to watch the sunset while getting further acquainted.

6

"Can I ask you a question and get a straight up answer? " Diamond asked Note.

"Definitely," Note answered, anticipating what was coming.

"You stuntin' pretty hard. How are you able to afford all of this? And please, don't lie to me, Note. I can't stand liars."

"I'll answer in part now, and in part when the time is ripe. Fair enough?"

"I guess that's acceptable, but it seems to me you've already answered the part you wanna prolong for another time."

"I own multiple, successful businesses. Some in Chicago, and a few others in various states throughout the country."

"Okay. What kinda businesses? Wait, slow up – how old are you again?"

"I'm 21 years old. I own the freight company you know about, as well as an exclusive laundromat. Both are here in Chicago. I have a few in other states too."

"21 with six businesses and a Benz I've never heard of. Seriously, you *gotta* be in the game to be living like this, Note. I'm no dummy. *How* else does someone your age get all of that?"

Note laughed. "My father passed away when I was 17. He left me a decent inheritance and enough game to know what to do with it. I made smart investments and never looked back. The Brabus is my baby, it's Mercedes' pinnacle of luxury. I'm the only one in Chicago with this car. My freight company alone suffices to cover the lifestyle I live.

"I'm sorry for your loss. Oh Ok, that's nice."

"Thank you, I appreciate it. You was signing up for college?"

"Yea. My goal is to become a RN, so I'm scheduled to begin my pre-med classes in the Fall. I wanna leave Chicago for a better life. I haven't thought much beyond that honestly, cause those are the things that matter most to me."

"A registered nurse, huh? That's good. Don't just settle for a RN tho, consider being a traveling nurse. You'll make more money and have more life experiences, and get more time for yourself if desire."

"Impressive. You know your stuff. I'll for sure keep that in mind and look into it. Thank you for sharing," Diamond said.

Note checked the time on his Audemars Piguet watch as the sun began its graceful descent over the lake. "We should leave now so we can catch this next reservation before I have to take you home."

Several minutes later, Diamond and Note walked into the Shanghai Palace, Chicago's number one Chinese restaurant. They were checked in promptly and escorted to their outdoor balcony table overlooking the City's magnificent skyline. The sun was still setting, so the weather was comfortable with a gently blowing breeze that faintly moved Diamond's hair.

Shortly after being seated at the candlelit table, a tall and curvaceous Thai waitress with long hair approached, slid two menus onto the table, and warmly introduced herself to the couple. "Good evening, my name is Amara and I'll be serving you two this evening. Can I get you something to drink?"

Note took the lead and answered, "Yes, two glasses of ice water will be enough for now. Thank you."

A couple of minutes later, Amara returned carrying her platter that contained two glasses of ice water and two bundles of silverware, which she subsequently laid on top of the burgundy table linen. Afterward, Amara made eye contact with both customers and in her soft, nearly childlike voice asked if they were ready to order or if they needed more time.

"More time, please," Note replied.

"No problem. Take your time and feel free to flag me if I haven't returned when you're ready."

Note and Diamond looked through the menu for several minutes before he broke the silence. "Anything pique your interest?"

"I've never tasted anything on this menu except lobster, and I'm sure what I had at Red Lobster can't compare to this 'Maine Lobster in its shell with ginger garlic sauce'. But I don't want to order anything with garlic. I know that much." She giggled.

"Bet. I got this." Note motions for Amara.

Amara approached the table and inquired, "Ready to order?"

"I believe so. We're gonna have twin orders. The traditional Peking duck with virgin lychee mojitos, please."

After Amara concluded her notes for their order, she confirmed Note's order by reciting it back to him. "Is that correct, sir?"

"Correct."

"And do you want the half or full duck on each order?"

"The half duck should be more than enough."

"Can I get you anything else?"

"That'll be it for now."

While they awaited their meals, the couple engaged in more intellectual conversation, taking turns picking one another's brain while simultaneously evaluating if the other was worth investing their time and effort into.

Note intentionally took his time with dinner and dessert. He was a man of intuition. He was closely monitoring his frequencies with Diamond, unbeknownst to her, to determine if he'd spend any time with her beyond today. Although Note saw potential in Diamond, that alone wasn't enough for her to secure a place in his life.

After finishing their Shanghai adventure, Note checked the bill resting inside the small fold on the table nearest him, reached in his back pocket for his wallet, pulled out his company Amex credit card along with a fifty-dollar bill, and tucked both inside the fold for Amara's retrieval. Immediately thereafter, Amara retrieved the fold from the table. and returned to her cash register to process the payment and pocket her tip. Moments later She returned quickly with the credit card and sat some breath mints on the table.

Note placed his credit card back in his wallet, then grabbed Diamond's hand. "I should get you home before it gets too late."

Note made his way to the Dan Ryan expressway. He opened the sunroof halfway, turned on Jeff Golub's Temptation album, and jumped on the expressway real smoothly. The Brabus took command of the on-ramp and Note merged to the carpool lane as he pressed the gas to 70 mph and then set it to cruise control.

Diamond sunk into the soft, yet firm leather seats and gripped the door handle to brace for the power of the speed. They cruised until Note reached Diamond's house.

There were no available parking spots on the block, so Note parked directly in front of her house and hopped out, meeting her in the front of the car. Diamond had her purse and shopping bag in her left hand and extended her right hand to Note, so he could escort her to the door.

Note scoped out a couple of thugs posted on either side of Diamond's block staring in their direction.

"Stay behind me in case these fools try to get jiggy." He unfastened and clutched the Glock on his hip while watching the thugs watching them.

Note was no stranger to Chicago's trenches. It's why they called this section of Chicago the 'Wild 100s'. Chicago goons practiced running down on unknown faces in their hoods, especially one's driving a luxury car like he was.

Diamond immediately provided Note with assurance. "If they were gonna do something to you, they would've got down on us when we hit the corner, not after I got out the car with you. They're security for they Mob. When you hit that corner, they saw and recognized my face, so you good, relax."

"I know why they posted. They don't call this the Wild 100s for nothing. I only relax in places of comfort, shordy. Da 100s ain't one of those places."

The couple walked to Diamond's porch, but Note didn't climb any of the stairs that led to the front door. Instead, he let Diamond walk up two of the steps, then spun her around. She wrapped her arms around

Note's neck. "I *had* a *really* great time with you, Note, seriously. Thank you for everything," she said sincerely. "I truly appreciate the experience, your time, and conversation. If there's a next time for us, your money and credit card will stay in your pockets, that's not what I'm about."

"It's good, beautiful. You're more than welcome. I'm glad we could enjoy today together. Thank you for your time and the opportunity to give you a *taste* of Chicago. I look forward to spending more time with you. Please understand, as a businessman, my schedule is often chaotic, but I'm willing to make time for you when our schedules permit."

"You're welcome as well. I'm also looking forward to getting to know you better. Get home safely, Note. Hopefully, I'll talk to you again before the night's over. If not, there's always tomorrow." She hugged him tightly and kissed his cheek before making her way up the remaining steps and going inside.

7

Monday, September 4, 2023

As Diamond drove into the parking lot of Jewels she realized she'd just had another unsolicited daydream. Years earlier, with the help of her parents, Diamond sought professional help with these occurrences. Her efforts landed her in the office of Uthman Tourè, one of Chicago's top psychiatrists.

After six months of weekly appointments with Dr. Tourè, Diamond was formally diagnosed with Post Traumatic Stress Disorder because of her intrusive flashbacks that would randomly be triggered. The flashbacks were all related to her experiences with Note.

Dr. Tourè's options for Diamond were psychotropic medication or to just live through the experiences. Diamond was adamant about not taking any meds, so she chose her latter option and has been living with these intrusive flashbacks ever since. For Diamond, they didn't cause any negative impact in her daily life;

they were more of an inconvenience than anything else since they were uncontrollable, but she was determined to survive without the side effects of any medication.

***

The bell rang to signal the end of first period at Julian High School. The hallways filled like a released dam. Students hung out for chatter while others made their way to their next class. Some students purchased small quantities of drugs. Nobody went to lockers to drop off or pick up books like other schools—lockers at Julian were banned years ago due to them being repeatedly used to stash drugs, guns, or other weapons.

Man was gliding through the hallway flirting and chatting with various young ladies that were interested in or sweating him. While he was engaged in small talk with a groupie, he was put in a headlock by his childhood best friend, Larry, known as "L". As he secured Man in a headlock, he said in his ear, "You lackin', Gang. Quit trippin' on these broads, bro." L let Man go. They slapped and shook hands before embracing.

"What you on, G?" Man asked.

"It ain't nun fool. What's da deal?"

"Jus coolin' bro, bout ta bank up in dis class in a second."

"Bro, yo goofy ass always runnin' to these classes like they paying you or sumn'."

"They paying me enough book knowledge to do what I need to do to get my family out da City. I got all these D-1s looking and getting at me. This my ticket, straight up. I keep tellin' yo ass I'm tired of Chicago. Just last night they was shootin' behind da crib, woke me and my OG outta a dead ass sleep," Man said, recalling the events. "My OG upped a pipe I ain't even know she had, and a stud came running past my window. *Who* in they right mind wanna live like that?"

"Aye!" L said rashly. "I needta holla at you, Gang. Let's push," L continued as he wrapped his arm around Man's shoulder and pulled him to walk together. The two of them walked until they were alone.

"What's up bro, what you tweakin' on?" Man asked.

L looked around and ensured they were alone. "Aye bro, on da Mob this don't go *NOWHERE* bro, straight up."

"Fa sho. My word, G."

"Bro, that was Knock-Knock last night. Da Mob had 'em smoke Money for snitchin' on TJ. We had a meeting last week. TJ sent paperwork with one of da guys that made bail last week. Bro said he blessed him wit da Mob's signature... one headshot and four to da body."

Man stood in complete shock as he replayed the events in his mind and counted the number of shots he heard—it was *five,* just like L said. Maybe L just heard and counted the shots too. He stayed on Peoria, one block away from Man.

"L, you loafin' right now?"

"Naw bro. I wouldn't play like that, bro. KK got low dis mornin'."

"Damn! That's bogish as heck, straight up. That's why I could *never* plug in wit any of y'all. It's all fu. I get he snitched and had it coming 'cause that's da rules y'all play by, but his best friend tho?!"

The bell rang for second period. Man looked L in the eyes. "I gotta go, Gang. I'll get up wit you at lunch or sumn'."

"Aight, bet. Love, Gang."

"Love, bro. Be safe."

Fifteen minutes before class would let out for lunch, Man pulled out his cellphone and sent a text.

"Pick me up at my class."

Within seconds, his phone lit up to notify him of the incoming text.

Bea: "k"

The message caused him to smile with pride. Brandiss, a 5'8" young lady with a slim, thick physique; D-cup breasts; and flawless chocolate skin with brown freckles glossing her face. She had a mesmerizing smile that hid a set of pearly white teeth. Her natural hair was long. Man knew he had her in pocket, despite having no serious interest in her. Ironically, she was the girl that everybody wanted.

When it was time for lunch, Man slowly gathered his belongings into his book bag, leaving Bea in the hallway waiting for him. He was third to last to step out of the classroom. The instant he entered the hallway, Bea showed a visible sign of relief coupled with a slight smile. Seeing Bea's response, Man got his confirmation that his plan was successful—to get Bea to fall deeper for him. Unbeknownst to him, Man possessed several of Note's traits, although the two never met.

Bea, like Man, was a senior at Julian. The two of them had been talking for a couple months and he had her wide open while consciously keeping his feelings reserved. He often would avoid her or intentionally let her see him talking to other ladies to make her pursue him more. He was enthralled by her attention and efforts. Man's paramount focus, however, was graduating and getting a full-ride scholarship to a D-1 school accompanied by a guaranteed starting running back position. He yearned to go pro and get his family out of the trenches, permanently.

Man approached Bea in the hallway and gave her a semi-tight hug, and hurling at her "What's up shordy, how are you?"

Bea hugged Man back. "Hiiii."

During their tenure, Bea learned Man was a health fanatic. He strongly believed in taking care of his body. Bea reached into her bag and said, "I brought you something." She pulled out a bag of raw almonds and a cold bottle of Powerade.

Man accepted the gifts with a smile on his face, then kissed her on the cheek. "Thanks, you didn't have to do that tho." Man admired Bea's simple, yet thoughtful gestures. It told him she not only was into him, but that she actually paid attention. He didn't have to explain certain things to her, like him being a health nut.

Bea smiled, showing the dimples imprinted between her lips and cheeks. "You're welcome."

Man spent lunch with Bea, making small talk and laughing with her. Man eloquently used his charm on Bea, opening her up in ways she'd yet experienced.

After school, Man went to the gymnasium's locker room to prepare for football practice. These were the only lockers usable to Julian students because they were under the direct control of the school's athletic coaches, and were only used during sports practice or actual games. Man went to his respective locker after the Coach unlocked the heavy-duty key lock on it, changed his clothes for practice, and placed all of his belongings in the locker before he locked it closed.

Once the entire team changed into their practice attire, they marched out to the field in unison for practice. Head Coach Lawrence Skinner, or Coach Law as he was often called, called the team together for an informative team meeting. "Everyone gather around!" he yelled. The team formed a circle around him as they each took a knee.

"Listen up. Today we're gonna have a somewhat intense practice, so I hope all of y'all are hydrated and sober. I want everyone to show up. As you can see in the bleachers, we have some visitors with us today, scouts from some D-1 colleges to see what some of y'all got. If you're not already on their radar, now is your chance to get noticed and start building connections for your future. We're starting with our routine warm-up, then lining up the offensive and defensive starting lineup to run the plays we've been working on, on both sides of the ball to show these gentlemen what we got." Coach looked his players in their eyes, continuing, "I don't want no slouching today, I want effective execution, and if you can't bring me that you'll be benched and replaced with your backup. This isn't just an opportunity for y'all, it's also an opportunity for me to get a better job and get da heck up outta da ghetto too, so make me look good."

In unison, the team and coaching staff shouted, "Break!" They dispersed.

Coach Skinner blew his whistle. "Alright gentlemen, let's go! Break me off 4 laps to warm up the muscles. Then we're gonna break off 100 jumping jacks; our body stretches; 100 push-ups in 4 sets of 25; 50 in-place leg raises and 100 squats. Then I want our starters lined up at the rock to run these routes. And remember, no man left behind. Let's *get it*! Team captains, run yo squad."

Within forty-five minutes, the Julian Jaguars varsity football team was done with warm-ups and the starting line-ups were on either side of the ball at the 50-yard line.

The coaching staff were on the sideline signaling plays and defenses with their hands like professionals with no verbal communication, as if it were a live game. Coach Skinner knew the scouts were primarily there to observe Man. However, the Coach wasn't partial to his team; he wanted to get all of his players on some college scout's radar. Therefore, he applied pressure to bring out the best in everyone.

For a straight hour, the Jaguar coaching staff had their players run plays alternating between the starting lineup and second-string players. The entire time, Man was in his head, pushing himself beyond his best. Although he didn't know what schools the recruits were from, he was confident they were there for him, and he wanted his skills to convince scouts he was not only an asset worth a full ride but also a guaranteed starting position.

The players executed the called plays with precision like it was a championship game; they were dominating on both sides of the ball. At running back, Man ensured he put up at least 7 yards every time he touched the ball. During this practice, Man touched the ball thirty times because their run-game was their strength, and he had no dropped balls.

When practice ended, the scouts formally introduced themselves to the team and commended the players and coaches for today's performances and their well-going season. The scouts then met with players of interest individually on the field, where each player was given the scout's business cards, and the scouts collected each players contact info. Man's self-motivation paid off. He was the only player that all three scouts talked to.

After wrapping up with the scouts, Man went back to the locker room. Once his locker was open, he pulled out his cellphone and texted Diamond.

"Mom, can you be here in 20-30 minutes? I wanna shower first."

Mom: "I'm already here. Meet me in the parking lot by the field when you're done."

"Okay."

8

When she got off work, Diamond went home and put some seasoned salmon in the oven to bake along with some fresh broccoli in a pot to lightly boil while she showered and changed clothes before picking Man up from practice.

When Diamond and Man got home from his practice, she had dinner ready for the two of them. She no longer had to tell seventeen-year-old Man to wash his hands after coming into the house as she did for several consecutive years prior. Man had deeply ingrained in him Diamond's passion for cleanliness. After they washed their hands and got settled, Diamond fixed their plates, and they had dinner together as usual.

"How was your day son" Diamond asked.

"It was aight. I'm dumb exhausted tho. I had three recruiters today. I turnt up, mom! Thirty runs, no dropped balls, and I put up at least 7 yards every play Coach said."

"Good job Man. I got there a little late, but I was checking you out from the visitors' bleachers. You did your thang son-son. So where were the recruiters from?"

"University of Illinois, Northwestern University, and DePaul University."

"Ok, locals. Are they of interest to you?"

"Not really. I've heard better talk from some of the top D-1s that I've already visited. I'm still unsure what I wanna major in, that's gonna weigh on my decision as well. I'm not shirting at all my freshman year, so if I'm not guaranteed a starting position, there's nothing to talk about. If I gotta work overtime to get my spot, I will, but I refuse to ride anyone's bench."

"To keep it a hunnid Mom, I'm leaning more towards a HBCU. I need to start hitting their coaches with my film to start getting offers from them, that's where my heart is."

Three Years Prior

Since his freshman year Man aspired to be the next Bo Jackson, Barry Sanders, or Marshawn Lynch—a beast running back who also had the ability to dominate baseball if necessary. His heart was in football although he knew he could make much more money in the MLB. Football gave him opportunities baseball didn't—to secretly take out all of his hidden pains, frustration, etc. on his opponents on the field through physical contact with no concerns of retaliation or being penalized. This was his one of his keys to success, and nobody, not even Diamond, knew he was harboring these feelings because he kept it all pinned in except on the field.

Man was only 5'10" and 155 pounds without an ounce of fat on him entering high school, yet he was fearless on the field. He was known for going head-to-head with even the biggest defensive linemen and linebackers, which, coupled with his speed and ability to cut quicker than an opponent can blink, made him a standout player since he started high school. Early on, his coaches would complain about his weight and muscle mass, and sometimes even benched him for stronger, heavier teammates.

The summer after his freshman year, Man successfully convinced Diamond and his grandparents to pay for him a yearly gym membership with a personal trainer to help him put on weight and muscle without taking away from his speed and ability to juke his opponents. Man devoted five days a week over the summer to working out; jogging Lakefront Trail; and changing his diet to accomplish his goal of getting bigger and stronger. He also spent countless hours watching exclusive running back highlights to learn moves and techniques.

When junior varsity tryouts came around in his sophomore year, Man managed to get his weight to 175 pounds and his was body was pure, sculpted muscle from his shoulders to his calves. Nobody on the defense could stop him and he put all the tryout running backs to shame.

After a single week of tryouts, the JV head coach, Sean Brown, called Man into his office after practice. He began the clandestine meeting by first giving Man his flowers for putting on weight and muscle while getting a couple of seconds faster over the summertime, then he asked Man pointedly "no pun intended, but have you started using steroids?"

Impulsively, Man began replying "*what* da …" before catching himself. He then adamantly countered "*hell nawww* I ain't on no damn steroids" in his Chicago drawl. "No pun intended, but have you started smokin' crack, Coach" Man shot back.

"Malik, I didn't mean to offend you. In my 15 years of coaching, I've never seen anyone make the kinda transition you have, especially in the time you did. I know you were upset by some of our calls last year concerning you, but again, I'm completely stunned by your progress, which is why we're here now."

"Coach, I appreciate it. I admit, you ridin my weight and size touched a nerve, but I was able to suck it up and move forward. However, being benched to have Brandon replace me due to his size despite him being slower and less agile than me left me *salty* and I used those experiences and feelings to fuel my motivation to not let it happen again."

"That's good, and the kinda attitude you needta have if you wanna succeed at the next level. I'm proud of you. That said, I think you deserve a shot at being promoted to varsity. I can't think of any defensive player in the City at JV that'll be able to handle you. With your progress and drive I believe you'll thrive at varsity. It'll also give you the opportunity to grow, improve, and get on recruiter radars. So, if you're up for the challenge, on Monday you can join the varsity tryouts with Coach Skinner and see where you fit in. I've already contacted the Coach about you last night and he assured me the door is open for you if you wanna go for it."

Internally, Man was celebrating like the Bud parade, but externally he showed minimum reaction by revealing a simple smile before calmly saying "wow, Coach. I appreciate it and you. I'll be there Monday."

"Good, I'm glad to hear this. If things don't work out for you at varsity, you're always welcome to come back here and I'll reserve your spot until you know your direction. I know you'll be good at varsity though. I'll notify Coach Skinner to be expecting you Monday."

As Man was leaving Coach Brown's office, the Coach called out "Malik."

"Sup Coach?"

"Go up there and leave your imprint, you're ready for whatever they throw at you!"

"Thanks Coach."

From that Monday in his sophomore year through his senior year, Man was the starting running back for the Jaguars.

9

September 2023

Despite being childhood best friends in high school, Man and L were growing apart. Man was deep into sports and determined to make a life for himself and his family, so he also immersed himself in school. L was devoted to the streets and everything that came with it. He wasn't on track to graduate and could care less. His only goal was to be someone within the Vicelord mob who would be well respected.

When Man wasn't in school, practicing, playing football, working out, doing homework, or gaming up girls, he was putting together highlight reels for Hudl and sending college coaches direct messages on social media. After making it to the varsity Jaguars in his sophomore year, Man busied himself in a fashion that'd keep him out of trouble.

Saturday, September 23, 2023

It was the biggest regular season game Julian had. The battle of the 100s, Christian Academy Fenger v. Julian. Kickoff was at 9 am on Saturday to deter gang violence that often accompanied Friday night games in Chicago. From experience, this game always sold out and had Chicago Police Department officers present regardless of where or when it was played.

Despite being played in the daytime and heavy police presence, metal detectors were present as well to prevent weapons from being brought into the game. All attendees, except CPD were required to pass through the metal detectors to enter the stadium.

The game started slow with the first half ending with a score of 7-14 in favor of the Jaguars. However, the second half quickly proved to be different. Julian successfully completed an on-sidekick at the start of the third quarter. The first play of Julian's possession was Man running for a 5-yard slant pass just beyond the line of scrimmage, relying on two of his wide receivers to block for him. Man ran 25-yards down the sideline before being forced out of bounds.

Coach Skinner hand signaled multiple times to his offensive lineup like the communication from a catcher to his pitcher. The quarterback, Mikey Williams, walked towards his position and held his crossed arms in the air with his hands forming zeros. *"Snake eyes, snake eyes!"* he yelled, stationing himself in a crouched form behind his center. Hearing the play call, Man's entire being flooded with emotion–the Coach had called Man's favorite play, one specifically designed for him to shine. Mikey looked around reading the defense, and intentionally waited a few seconds for the crowd to quiet so that the only thing to be heard was the Fenger cheerleaders shouting in the background.

As everything settled, Mikey growled. *"Set, HUT!"* The play was in motion. The Jaguars' offensive line did their job and spread the defensive line to the left and right like Moses did the Red Sea. Mikey spun to his right and put the ball directly in Man's center grasp.

He clutched the ball between his arms. Launching forward like an unstoppable Hummer, he burst through the gaping hole made by his O-line. Man scanned the field as he traversed it. He spotted an oversized linebacker who locked eyes with him, vigorously propelling himself directly in his direction. Man began chanting aloud, "Bo, Barry, Marshawn … Bo, Barry, Marshawn." This incantation reminded him of not only who inspired him to be great, but also to ponder what they would do in that moment. Seconds moved faster than light as Man weighed his options. He clutched the ball tighter to prevent a fumble, then slightly dropped his helmet to land in the linebacker's chest. The impact was loud and was followed by a crunching noise that echoed throughout the stadium. The linebacker was laid out.

In sync with the linebacker's failure, the Jaguars' fans released a uniform of *ooohhh's*. Man continued treading center field like he owned it. Seeing this, a middle linebacker and cornerback for Fenger pursued him. With his teammate being heavier and slower, the cornerback, who was much lighter and quicker, easily closed in on Man, prompting him to slant left to maintain distance until he reached the end zone for his second touchdown. The Jaguars crowd erupted in cheers and standing ovation for Man. The commentator celebrated over the PA system. "W*hatta play*! A 23-yard run by the Jaguars running back, Malik Willaims for his second touchdown of the game!"

The Jaguars feasted on Fenger's Titans by ending the game 35-7. In the second half, Man scored three touchdowns with 250 rushing yards. Tensions were high. There were a couple of containable fights on and off the field, and there was no casualties. Everyone was able to leave and return to their respective destinations.

After showering, getting dressed, and getting in the car with Diamond, Man pulled out his cellphone and turned it on. After entering his unlock code, notifications of messages, tags, emails, and DMs poured in.

Man checked his texts first. He had messages from university coaches who were interested in recruiting him. He checked his tags next and learned he was tagged by a local photographer. One of his groupies voluntarily attended the game and snapped several pictures of him on the field and a couple of him on the sideline with his helmet off she posted. Next, he checked his Twitter DMs, and to his surprise; he had a reply from 6 of the 10 HBCU coaches he reached out to. Each head coach and/or offensive coordinator advised Man they'd reviewed his Hudl film, performed additional research on him, thanked him for reaching out to them, and each expressed their interest and requested he provide his contact information.

"Mama!!!! Six!!!!" Man exclaimed.

Puzzled, Diamond inquired, "*Six* what baby?"

"*Six* HBCU coaches got back at me. I hit ten of them. Oh, my God! I'm finally getting what I want. This is a dream come true. I'm going even harder now. I'm gonna hit more coaches than I did the first time. I'm telling you, I'm getting a full ride to a HBCU and I'm gonna *turn up* for them, straight up."

"*Congratulations,* son. I'm proud of you. So how many schools is that now?"

"13. 7 regular D-1s and 6 HBCU D-1s."

"Wow Man, that's good, baby. I haven't seen you this excited over any of the schools since you got your first few, but even then, you wasn't *this* happy."

"Yeah. Like I said, I'm concrete on HBCUs. I just gotta find a school with a decent academic program that'll also guarantee me a starting position."

"I understand, son. Man, I just want you to know how proud I am of you and the young man you're growing into. *Nobody* in the family has done the things you have and are doing. Although my knowledge of your father's side is limited, I'm unaware of anyone in his family that's done it either."

The mere mention of Note was a sensitive topic for Man, regardless of who brought it up. He never met the man and only knew that he passed away from a heart attack before he was born.

"Since you brought up his family, Mama, keep it 100, why you haven't introduced me to his family or put us in contact so that I can get to know them?"

"I don't know where to find your grandmother. Your grandfather passed away before I met your father, and your aunt and her children are all in the game in some form or another—the very thing I've been striving diligently to keep you away from."

Not knowing what to say, Man sat quietly staring down at his phone as he continued scrolling.

Diamond drove into her detached garage through the alley behind their house and parked. Seeing Man's energy change, Diamond asked him if he was okay.

In a low tone, Man replied, "Yeah, I'm good."

Diamond's heart sank. She hurt for her son, but she wouldn't show him. She gently grabbed Man's chin and turned his head towards her. "Didn't I teach you to look people in their eyes during conversation?"

Man looked his mother in her brown, almond shaped eyes. "Yes, ma',am."

"I'm sorry for all the hardship you've had to endure. I'm sure you have feelings I can't completely understand, especially given I haven't had to experience all the things you have. But please understand that I've done and will continue to do my best for you--mentally, physically, and emotionally. I'm not perfect, nor do I know everything. Just trust me. Trust my decisions. And I'm gonna keep my part of the deal and tell you everything about your father when you graduate."

"Aight mom."

Diamond kissed Man's cheek. "I love you, son."

"I love you too."

Diamond pressed the button on her genie to close the garage door, and they got their belongings and entered the house.

10

In his room, Man was watching recorded highlights of Marshawn Lynch and taking written and mental notes of any and everything that stood out to him that he didn't already know. He'd been through these same highlights at least 10 times since he received the film a month ago, but he always found something he didn't catch previously. This was how he generally spent his time at home.

Man's concentration was broken by a sudden and unexpected 'ding-dong' sound that was rare in the Williams household. Without a shadow of a doubt, Man knew the door was for him or it was the local Jehovah's Witness members seeking to propagate to them for the next hour.

"I got it, Mama."

Man got off his bed, slid into his comfortable Nike flip-flops, and made his way to the door. He looked through the peephole without making any noise, just as

Diamond taught him over the years. L was standing on the porch.

Man unlocked and opened the front door then did the same on the metal screen door Diamond had installed years ago. He stepped out on the porch, shook hands and hugged L. "What's da deal, bro?"

"Ain't nun, jus coolin Gang. Stopped by ta check on you. What you on bro?"

"I was leaning back watching film bro, you know ion be on nun but sports, school, and girls. Straight up," Man said with slight laughter. "I'm tired as ion know what from da game, so I was just relaxing." Man took a few steps to his left and sat on the slab of concrete that similar homes used to hold flower pots.

Leaning against a smaller slab of concrete, L said, "I heard y'all tore dey ass up bro, and you went 10-5 crazy on 'em Joe."

"It was a good game, bro. No cap. They just couldn't handle our 2nd half pressure."

"Don't be playin' that calm, collect crap wit me, bro. I ain't no news reporter interviewing yo ass. Did you turn up or what? One of da guys told me you did yo duggy, on gang."

"Why you ain't come check me out? If you would've popped out like yo guy did, you'd know how I did. Straight up." Man shot back intentionally being a smart ass.

"C'mon G, you know I ain't missing no home games unless I got sumn' to do. I had packs to move for da Mob, I'm tryna put a lil paper in my pocket. So did you get busy or what?"

"Straight up tho, I did my duggy Gang, no cap. Three touchdowns and 250 rushing yards. The energy was different today, something I can't explain. From the minute I stepped on the field, I felt something I never have, and it was like that the whole game, bro."

"Damn! You went 10-5 crazy fa real, Gang," L said excitedly as he shook Man's hand.

"Thanks, bro. But you know I ain't wit nun of that gang shit."

"I know, bro, but you from 10-5 if you plugged or not, and can't nobody take that away from you. You been here since you came from the hospital. Most of these studs from the block moved here, ya dig, so you *always* 10-5 in my eyes," L reminded him. "Let's slide up to Jed's right quick. I'm low-key hungry."

"Aight, lemme put my shoes on and grab my phone."

Man went to his room and threw on his Nike Vapormax Plus shoes, grabbed his phone off the bed, and pocketed a few dollars he had sitting on the dresser. On his way outside, Man texted Diamond: "Mom, I'm going to Jed's with L, be back in a minute."

Mom: "Okay, be careful."

Man and L walked down S. Sangamon to 105th, then made their way to Jed's Fruit and Vegetables corner store. As they entered, the bell attached to the inside door handle rang, grabbing the store owner's attention. "W'sup Mr. Jed?" Both Man and L said.

"L, Man, how are you young men doing?" Mr. Jed asked excitedly from behind the plexiglass window covering his entire counter.

"All is well," L quickly replied to represent his gang affiliation.

This response caused Mr. Jed to stop smiling. He knew L and Man since they were born and watched both grow up throughout the tenure of his store. He knew L's fate was jail or premature death, neither of which he wanted for any of Chicago's youth, but with L's decision, it was inevitable. Mr. Jed continued, "Man, WGN aired the game live today. I watched y'all go to work. You had a heck of a game, congratulations! Whatever you're getting today, it's on me. It's the least I can do."

"That's what's up. Thanks, Mr. Jed." Man returned.

He and L walked down the snack aisle towards the drinks in the freezer at the back of the store. Man slowed down to grab some Hot and Spicy Jay's potato chips while L made his way toward the freezers.

L reached in the freezer and grabbed a cold Brisk Lipton Lemon Iced Tea. "You want a tea, bro?"

Just as Man turned in L's direction to answer, the bell tied to Jed's entrance rang out and all attention went in that direction. A man standing 5'11, and weighing 190 pounds with a muscular build stepped into Jed's store and locked eyes with Man and L. "Sup folks?"

Man knew their situation just turned bad, but he didn't have a clue what was to come. He broke eye contact with this grown man and turned his attention back to L. "Yeah, good look...." Man didn't finish his statement before he saw L's extended arm raise in the man's direction. Shots ring out.

Two shots echoed throughout the store and Man dropped the bag of chips he had in his hand. He stood frozen in complete shock. Mr. Jed instinctively ducked below the counter the instant he saw L's Glock 23 pointing at the victim. The muscular gang member dropped from the headshot. L walked towards his victim, looking at his body for any signs of life. He stood over the man with his pistol aimed at his chest, confirming his kill. "Let's get up outta here, Gang," L yelled to Man as he ran out of the store.

Man and L ran down 105th and split up at S. Green, where L went left down the alley until he reached his cousin's house. Man ran to his house down the S.

Sangamon alley, hopped the locked gate, and rested in the cement stairwell leading to the basement to catch his breath before going in the house. He entered the house through the back door attached to the kitchen, which was also closest to Diamond's bedroom.

Diamond heard his entrance from her bedroom and called out, "Man?"

"Yes, Mama?"

"Why you coming through the back, everything alright?"

"Everything good, Mama. I thought I dropped something in the backyard when me and you got home earlier, so I was checking," he lied.

Man went straight to his room. His heart was still pounding intensively as he sat on the edge of his bed with his door shut, staring into space, playing everything back. What he just experienced in Jed's had become ingrained in him against his wishes, he could see every detail in slow motion from the moment he heard the bell ring until the instant he exited the store behind L. He could hear the loud shots of L's Glock 23 as if he was standing next to the pistol when it was fired. He could smell the burnt gunpowder like he was the one standing behind the pistol. 'Folks' head exploded like a melon. Man had never witnessed a murder before, nor partook in any crime outside of stealing from Jed's when he was younger.

While playing everything over in his mind, he realized Jed had several small security cameras installed years earlier because of being robbed repeatedly. Man went into a full-fledged panic thinking about the cameras. Plus, Mr. Jed was an eyewitness. His first thought was to pack as much clothing as possible and get up with L for a spot to lay low. Surely the Mob would hide them both until the heat died down, *but* he's not a member and had no interest in becoming one. That's why he was in this jam now; gang activity.

Man was conflicted, angry, frustrated, and scared. He picked up his cellphone to call L for help, guidance, anything. Before he could finish unlocking his phone, Man remembered police technology could trace phone calls, and retrieve deleted texts and all. He slammed his phone into his mattress with a vigorous rage. "Dammit!" Man lacked answers and direction in this situation.

He laid back on his bed and crossed his arms over his face while trying to calm down, collect himself, and come up with a sound plan. He shut his eyes, took several deep breaths, and released each one in a slow, controlled manner until he felt his inner self becoming still. This tranquility was something he's never experienced before, yet it was comforting.

A little calmer, he felt he could process and think until just as he was gradually sorting his thoughts, this peace was broken by blaring police sirens in the distance. He knew exactly where they were racing–Jed's. Man got up and snuck out the back door. He exited the backyard and walked down the alley to 105th where he hid behind the corner house, looking straight at Jed's. Man saw two CPD cars, one unmarked Crown Victoria, and a van with a 'coroner' label on it. The two CPD cars had their blue light bars activated. An officer exited Jed's and popped the trunk on his CPD car to remove a big roll of yellow tape that had *POLICE LINE, DO NOT CROSS* stamped on it repeatedly in bold black letters.

The officer walked to the driver's side of his patrol car, tied the loose end of the tape around the external rear-view mirror then rolled it around the driver's side. He did the same to the back of the car and continued with the tape towards Jed's one-way entrance.

Heart thumping through his chest, Man ran back down the alley to his house.

11

Man began sorting through all of his thoughts, one at a time. For the first time in his life, he knew and understood definitively why Diamond had been emphasizing to him his entire life to stay away from gangs and gang members or anyone who wasn't doing anything positive with their life. She wanted him to avoid this *exact* or similar scenario – getting caught up in some BS in general, or in something that had absolutely nothing to do with him. Now he's in it, and knee deep.

What if I get arrested? What can they charge me with when I literally did nothing? What about graduation? College? My family gonna remain stuck in the damn trenches. His thoughts ran wild before two shots penetrated them. Suddenly, he was back in the store. Man tried to shake the feeling. "I ain't do *nothing*, ion got nun to worry about, straight up." He said aloud.

Man unlocked his phone and texted Diamond: "mom, what's for dinner?"

Immediately after sending that text, one came in. He thought it was Diamond replying, but it was Bea.

"Wyd?"

"Coolin, sup with you?"

"Nothing, just got back home. Somebody got killed at Jed's today, did you hear?"

Man's heart sunk into a baseless abyss as his biggest fear became a reality. Yes, he saw the coroner's van at Jed's, but he *hoped* that was a shooting protocol in case the victim is confirmed dead. He read the message three more times before replying.

"Fa real? How you know? Nah, I hadn't heard."

Amid the conversation with Bea, Diamond texted Man back, but he didn't open or read it. He wanted to get as much information as possible from Bea.

"I went to Jed's to get something to eat and couldn't get in the store. The police got it taped off, everybody out there, and there's a coroner van parked right there on Halsted. My friend said she heard the shots while getting her hair done in Niesha's next door."

Man's heart began racing again. He took his time texting her back. "Damn, that's cold. Lemme get back at you in a min, I gotta holla at my OG."

Man opened Diamond's text: "You feel like going to Harold's?"

Outside was the last place Man wanted to be. It'd be just his luck to go get some chicken and fries for him and his mom only to get arrested for murder and never make it back home.

"Naw Mama. Can you cook some teriyaki or Kung pao orange chicken, broccoli, and baked potatoes?"

"Okay, I'll get up in a minute."

***

L did his best to keep calm while at his cousin Tonya's house. He acted like he was coming by to check on his uncle and aunt. Tonya was home by herself lounging in some boxers and a tank top, talking to her friend on the phone.

"Sup cuz, whatchu doing" L asked Tonya when she answered the door and let him in.

"Hold on girl. Chilling, what's up with you?" Tonya responded as she walked back into the living room.

L walked into the kitchen and washed his hands to remove any gunshot residue, then opened the refrigerator for something cold to drink. "I ain't on nun, just came through to check on y'all for a minute. What happened to all da juice?"

"My mom and dad went shopping, they should be back in a little bit."

L joined Tonya in the living room and sat down on the couch opposite the single-seat recliner she was sitting in. L looked up at the flat screen TV mounted to the wall. Lil Durk's 'You Can't Run' video was playing.

Before Tonya got too deep in her gossip session on the phone, she was interrupted. "Aye cuz, swap phones wit me for a min please, I need to call Tyrone."

For a split-second, Tonya hesitated and looked puzzled, but then she remembered that Knock-Knock was on the run. "Bird, lemme call you back in a few minutes, alright?"

The two swapped phones, and as he began dialing Knock-Knock's number, he made his way outside for privacy. Turning back, L said, "Dollar sign, 2212, dollar sign."

"What?" Tonya questioned.

"Da code, T." L said as he walked through the front door to the porch.

"Yo," Knock-Knock answered.

"KK, what's da deal?"

"L?"

"Yeah."

"Why you callin' me from Tonya's phone, what's up?"

"Man Chālie, it's ugly. I got down on a stud today."

"WHAT?!? Say less. Pull up, we'll talk when you get here. Love," Knock-Knock said before hanging up.

L deleted Knock-Knock's number from Tonya's phone then went back inside and swapped phones back. "I'm up cousin, thanks. I love you," he said, hugging her.

"Love you too cuz, be safe."

***

When the Greyhound bus was pulling into the Gary, Indiana bus station, L pulled out his phone and texted Knock-Knock: "?". Seeing the text message on his phone, he knew L had arrived at the bus station in Gary, Indiana. Knock-Knock jumped into Cassie's 2022 Infiniti Q60 to go pick him up.

Ten minutes later, Knock-Knock was pulling into the bus station. He slowly cruised through the parking lot, looking around for his little brother. Knock-Knock had the sunroof open and both front windows down. It took all of two minutes to spot L's 5'7", 165 pound frame standing at a distance from everyone, looking around nervously. Knock-Knock blew the horn twice to get his attention.

L saw the car coming in his direction, but he couldn't see the driver through the front windshield. He instinctively put his right hand in his right pocket and clutched the Glock 23 he was still carrying, with a willingness to use it again. As the vehicle neared, L slightly bent over to look through the passenger side window frame. When he saw his big brother's face, he removed his hand from his pocket, walked towards the car, hopped in the passenger seat, and adjusted it to his comfort.

The car had an alluring cherry freshener smell and the royal blue interior was in flawless condition. The seats were the coziest L had experienced. He looked around the car from front to back in utter amazement. "What's da deal, KK?" L said as they completed their gang handshake.

"Coolin bro, what you on? You tweakin' in da streets now?"

"Man bro, it wasn't even like that. Dis fool came up in Jed's tweakin' so I got jiggy, straight up!"

Knock-Knock rolled the windows up and closed the sunroof. He turned on his THF Billa's playlist with 'Attention' playing first. They left the Greyhound parking lot and rode the main street. "So run it back to me. What happened?"

L told Knock-Knock the entire story from the moment he went to see Man to the point of him calling from Tonya's phone. Knock-Knock was impressed, shocked, and heartbroken all at once. He took in all of what L told him and could only blame himself for the path that L was on. His only brother was officially a stepper—a certified killer, and there was no turning back for either of them. "You sho he died?"

"Yep. I hit 'em in da head and when I went to him to finish him off, there was no sign of life in him. His brains was on da floor."

"Aight. He fa sho wasn't from Roseland cuz he would've known you my brother, and would've left y'all alone. We needta get you a new phone and number. Take yo SIM card out, break it, and toss it out da window. You still got da pipe?"

L destroyed and tossed the broken SIM as told. He reached in his right pocket, pulled out the Glock 23, and sat it on his lap showing Knock-Knock.

"Take da bullets out, wipe'em down, and look in the glove box for the latex gloves. Put the bullets in there for now. I'll hit Chief after we handle dis business, and put him on notice for any lickback ol boy folks might wanna get, and I'll also find out who dis fool was, where he was from, etc. In the meantime, you out here with me until I can figure things out. 12 gone put a warrant out for you once they get yo identity from Mr. Jed or the video."

"Who whip is dis, bro?" L asked, changing the subject.

"Cassie, my lil ridah. She solid, and we good out here. Nobody in da City know about her or that I be out here, *keep* it that way." Knock-Knock ended sternly.

"Bet. How you meet shordy?"

"She was in da City bussin' cards in da Gold Coast when I was doing some shopping. Thick ass white girl was standing on bidness. I saw her bust a play, and couldn't let her pass me without shootin' my shot. I instantly grabbed her hand and put it down. She picked up e'rythang I dropped, and it's been on since, straight up."

12

They pulled into a gated parking lot that contained three opened, industrial sized garage doors with a sign that read *Skip's Metal Refinery*. Inside, the building was dark except for lights at specified workstations and several visibly lit kilns. Once Knock-Knock parked, he told L, "Gimme the pipe." L surrendered the Glock 23. "Stay in da car. I'll be right back."

Knock-Knock put the Glock in his pocket and exited the Q60, then walked into the middle garage door, where he spotted who he was looking for. He walked up to the husky white man who was covered in tattoos from his neck as far down as the eyes could see. "Skip!" Knock-Knock called out. The 6" 200-pound man with a long, dingy beard turned around.

"KK, what's up, man?" The two shook hands firmly and Skip inquired, "business?"

"Indeed."

Knock-Knock then followed Skip to a set of stairs that led to Skip's office. Once inside, Knock-Knock closed the door behind him, then pulled out the Glock 23 and handed it to Skip with $500 cash. Skip put the pistol in his waist and pulled his t- over the pistol's butt, then folded the money into his pants pocket.

The couple went back downstairs to Skip's workstation, which already had a lit kiln going. Skip removed the Glock from his waist and placed the pistol inside a melting pot along with some scrap metal on top, then eased the melting pot inside the kiln for a few minutes. Skip removed it from the kiln and then showed Knock-Knock the bright orange liquid sitting in the melting pot.

"Good lookin'," Knock-Knock said to Skip, then went back to his car and drove to Lake Street Beach, where he dumped the bullets into his gloved hand and threw them into the water along with Man's broken cellphone.

On the way to the cellphone store, Knock-Knock looked at L and asked in a serious tone, "What's up with Man, what'd he do after y'all split up?"

"Ion know, haven't heard from him."

"You trust him to keep his mouth shut even if he's picked up by 12?"

"Yeah, that's bro. He not doin' no talkin'."

"L, he gotta lot going for himself, and you know how bad he wanna leave da City. I can't afford to lose you on a hunch, Gang, so if you think he gone possibly fold, now is da time to say so. I can have one of da guys smother him before 12 snatch'em up cuz they *gonna* get'em if he still in da hood. It's just a matter of time."

"Naw. Knock-Knock he good, trust me. His OG laced him when he was a shordy not to talk to or help 12. Leave'em alone, that's my guy."

"*Aight*" Knock-Knock said with hesitation. "I hope you right cuz if you not, he's gonna give you up and be a star witness against you."

After getting L a new phone, Knock-Knock drove to the Miller Beach suburbs and parked in the driveway resting on the side of a fenced, 1961 vintage, two-story house that rested on a one-acre plot of land. Externally, the house was a balanced blend of gray on the top portion of the house and white on the bottom.

Before getting out of the Infiniti, L looked around in awe considering this was his first time experiencing a neighborhood without narrow streets with cars parked on either side of the road; no gang security or drug dealers on the corners; no gunshots echoing in the air. He experienced total serenity without ever knowing what it was. L stepped out and looked around. One word flowed from his mouth, "Damn!" He felt safe and comfortable despite being there seconds. The only thing to be heard was chirping birds and a faint breeze.

Knock-Knock got out of the car and turned on the alarm after both front doors had been shut. Reading his little brother's mind, Knock-Knock said, "Much different than da crib, huh?"

"Man Joe, waayyy different."

"Actually, da City has many good parts. We just dealt the worst parts of it, unfortunately. Maybe when da heat cool down, I'll show you some better parts of da 'Raq, it's really not bad once you leave the trenches."

Knock-Knock led L to the back door of the house. "Lock da door behind you, Gang." They stepped into the mudroom of the house, removed their shoes, and sat them to the side with the others. They entered the back of the spotless kitchen.

Immediately to his left, L saw the pristine McNally 9-piece Marble Top Pedestal Dining set with high-backed, cream-colored chairs, with 5 perfectly dispersed white globe pendant lights throughout the kitchen. He noticed the Carrara, Italian white marble streaking gray against a minimal backdrop countertop, along with the island's matching countertop and black, cushioned bar chairs. Elegant White Shaker Kitchen Cabinets decorated the entire kitchen. L looked at the high end Miele 48" Steel Freestanding Dual Fuel Natural Gas Range and the Sub-Zero Pro 30.4 side-by-side Built-in Refrigerator with a Glass Door.

He took a step towards the Delta Rivet Workstation and Farmhouse Apron Front, Dual Bowl Kitchen sink to wash his hands. He couldn't help but inspect the smooth DuraLax-Vinyl—Alpine Frost Rigid Core floor beneath his feet. When he reached the sink after Knock-Knock, he placed his hands under the faucet with side sensors that turned the water on and off and washed his hands.

The kitchen alone was so mind-blowing that L hardly recognized the smell of the 'black butter' oil burning or two of the Valor speakers of the Legacy Audio system playing Ann Marie's 'E.V.O.L.' in the kitchen. L's tranquility was broken by Knock-Knock's voice. "Anytime you come in da house, Gang, use da back door. Leave your shoes in the mudroom, no shoes in da house, and *always* wash your hands when you come in before touching on stuff. As you see, we keep da crib clean. While you're here, I expect you to do your part, and Cassie will hold the rest down for us."

"Aight, I gotchu bro."

Just then Cassie entered the kitchen to greet Knock-Knock and meet his little brother. She was wearing snug fitting shorts that barely reached the middle of her thighs and a t-shirt that covered three-fourths of her ass. She walked up to Knock-Knock, wrapped her arms around his lower back, and greeted him. "Hey babe," then rose on her tiptoes to kiss him.

Knock-Knock extended his arm towards L, who was drying his hands with a hand towel given to him. "Cass, dis my lil brother, L. L, dis my woman, Cassie."

"Nice to meet you, L," Cassie said genuinely.

"Likewise, Cassie," L returned while trying not to give into his desire to take a long, hard look at her.

Cassie was Caucasian, with long black hair down the middle of her back. She stood 5'5" and weighed 150 pounds. She was a natural beauty and only wore lip gloss to accentuate her Madeline Kline sized lips. Her body was curvaceous. 34-22-39 measurements. She carried a butt like Amber Rose. Her stomach was flat and lightly sculpted. Her hips were undefinable, yet she had thighs like a gymnast and perfectly tanned skin.

"L got in a jam and needs to lay low for a while, so he'll be with us until further notice."

"No problem, baby. I just finished double-checking his room. In a little while I'll go grocery shopping because I've only been buying enough food for us. Did he bring any clothes with him?"

"Nah, he came as is. I'll take him shopping tomorrow," replied Knock-Knock.

"Okay. There's a few bands left on that Amex card, so you can use that."

"I'll get it from you later. That'll save me some money." Knock-Knock took L to his room before retreating to the living room to make some calls to Chicago.

13

Due to the murder that occurred in his store, Mr. Jed was forced to close early so the police could conduct their investigation. They questioned Mr. Jed, collected evidence, and removed the deceased from the store. Mr. Jed was also forced to stay late to clean up the mess left behind by L's actions—blood, drinks, and opened food on the floor resulting from the second shot that missed the deceased.

While cleaning up, Mr. Jed played everything over in his mind and found himself utterly heartbroken, not for his loss but the loss of three young men from his community who looked like him and had now been deprived of experiencing life from their poor decisions. Jed witnessed people throw away their lives over *absolutely nothing.* It was a senseless crime to him, and it didn't have to happen, indeed shouldn't have happened as far as he was concerned. At 58 years old, he'd watched each Chicago generation get worse than the one that came before it. That reality was disheartening, yet this is exactly why he moved his family out of the hood.

Although he maintained his businesses in urban Chicago, Mr. Jed used each day in his store as an opportunity to do good deeds in various ways hoping he could somehow change the narrative amongst his people.

The police pressed Mr. Jed repeatedly for the identities and/or addresses of the murder suspects. He reluctantly gave physical descriptions of the two people that fled the crime scene. Mr. Jed refused to give the names of L or Man because he didn't want to help law enforcement ruin either of their lives, although L had already done so for both of them. Mr. Jed was well aware of L's affiliation; as well as Knock-Knock's reputation and inclination for violence. He was unwilling to jeopardize his or his family's lives through retaliation.

Even when the investigating detectives threatened Mr. Jed with being charged with obstruction of justice, that wasn't enough to make him break. His life was worth more to him than a few hours in lock-up. Being a serial entrepreneur and having over 30 years of successful business, Mr. Jed had more than enough money to hire the best attorney in town to fight any charges they threw his way. He also knew law enforcement would be back on Monday with a warrant to sieze his security footage. Mr. Jed wouldn't give it up without one. This was not just for his protection, but also to help Man and L buy some time to get out of town.

***

"Man!" Diamond yelled from the kitchen as she sat the plates on the table. There was no answer. Diamond yelled louder. "Mannn!" Nothing. "Ugggh," she huffed, walking to his room. Diamond opened Man's bedroom door, stepped partly inside, and shouted.

Man arose and gasped for air. He heard that 'hey' loud and clear, and thought it was the police coming to arrest him. His heart was beating rapidly once again. Seeing his mom and not an officer gave Man instant relief. "Yeah, Mama," he answered.

"Dinner ready. Get up." Diamond closed his door and returned to the kitchen.

Man sat up and slipped his feet into his Nike slippers then stretched to shake off the sleep and near heart attack he thought he'd just experienced. He got up and walked to the kitchen to have dinner with his mother after a long day.

Diamond knew her son better than anyone. Not only did she carry him in her body for nine months and gave birth to him, but for the last 17 years, she's spent every day learning him. There wasn't much, if anything, he could hide from her. She poured drinks for them. Diamond asked Man straight up, "What's wrong, son?"

"Nothin Mama," he answered dully.

Man wanted badly to open up to his mother and get her advice on what he should do, but he knew she'd be disappointed in him and definitely upset. A long lecture about what she's been telling him his entire life would surely follow. That's not what he wanted, so he kept his dilemma to himself.

"Are you sure, Man? You've been off since you came back from the store," pressed Diamond.

Diamond's last three words sent chills over Man's entire body. He looked down and picked through his food. "Yeah, I'm good."

When they finished their food, Diamond got up and walked over to Man, kissed his cheek, and hugged him tightly, hoping to provide him consolation and space to open up with her about whatever he was going through. "Goodnight, I love you son-son," she said before going to her room to get ready for bed.

"I love you too. Goodnight, Mama."

14

Monday, September 25, 2023

First thing Monday morning, Detectives Raymond Simmons and Joey Goodman were in the judge's chambers with a computer-generated search warrant for the video footage from Jed's security cameras, inside and outside of the store prior to, during, and after the murder of Christopher McCarren.

After reviewing the warrant's details and lawful basis to ensure all technicalities were met, the judge went straight to the signature line and signed his name with no qualms. The detectives took the warrant, had the court clerk photocopy it, and drove to Jed's store with determination.

Mr. Jed saw the unmarked Crown Victoria with two white men occupants coming down Halsted while he was doing his ritual sweeping around his entrance and setting up his sale sign outside. He was expecting their return. Both Detectives were eager to bury L and Man in prison.

The detectives' unmarked car parked in front of Jed's. Two cheaply suited detectives with an aura of confidence stepped out. "Morning, Mr. Jed," said Goodman as he handed him some folded papers. "Your copy of the signed warrant for your security footage of the events given rise to the murder of Christopher McCarren on Saturday."

Mr. Jed stopped what he was doing and glanced over the paperwork, then entered his store with the Detectives on his heels. "Wait here," Mr. Jed said as he went through a door that led to the back of his store.

He went to the counter and reached to a shelf underneath, then deposited a paper-covered CD into the bulletproof item box he had installed years ago.

"That's your copy, keep it, and get the heck out of my store," he said distastefully as he pushed the box out for them to retrieve the disc.

Detective Goodman grabbed the disc and put it in his inside blazer pocket.

"Thank you for your service, sir," Detective Simmons sarcastically said.

The Detectives raced back to their car, made a U-turn, then sped towards the expressway so they could return to their office and go through this video footage to see what actually transpired and help them identify their fugitive suspects.

***

Knock-Knock had touched basis with the Chief of Roseland's Vicelords, gave him the rundown about what happened with L, and the potential for backlash on the Mob once the facts had come out. The Chief was able to give Knock-Knock an update on the situation as well. L was right, ol' boy didn't survive the headshot. No Good, his name in the streets—wasn't from Roseland as Knock-Knock suspected, and was a Black Disciple from a different part of the 100s. Apparently No Good thought he'd caught some Gangster Disciples, their arch enemy, slipping in the store. Man made it to his crib safely, and as of that Monday, hadn't been picked up by 12.

The whole Mob was on high alert, and the Roseland community was notified about the pending war and to keep any innocent bystanders out the way.

Knock-Knock went to L's room and shared all that he learned. He also used this as an opportunity to have the heart-to-heart he knew was necessary. Knock-Knock looked his little brother in the eyes to read him. "How you holding up, Gang, seriously?"

"I'm good bro, on Gang. Why you tweakin'?"

"L, listen, taking a human life isn't easy, and once you do it, especially at your age, it brings a different kinda animal out of you, there's no turning back, you can't bring that person back. 1 of 2 things gone happen, you gonna go harder meaning killin' gets easier for you or you wind up regretting your actions through empathy, and it ends up haunting you." He paused. "I was your age when I caught my first body, and keeping it a hunnid with you, regardless of which side of da coin you fall on, catching a body messes with yo head, straight up, ion care who you are. Ya know I'ma *certified* steppa bro, Money was my third. When you take a life, you *don't* remain da same, Gang, and more times than not it's da 1st body that bothers people most, so I'm checking on you to make sho you straight."

"KK, check it out. You confirmed it, buddy was strapped and lookin' for smoke. If I didn't do my duggy in there, we wouldn't be havin' dis conversation right now. You prolly would be in da City hunting for ol' boy and planning my funeral. *You* taught me to stand on bidness, I did that. I ain't for *nun,* Knock-Knock."

"L, you did exactly what you should have, and I'm glad you stood on bidness. However, it doesn't make it easier for me to know I turnt you out. It actually *hurts* to know I'm da reason your life is what it is. I never wanted you in this. I always thought you and Man would push each other right into da pros together. But we're here now, and I just want you to know I'll be here when you need me."

I understand big bro, and I appreciate it. As of now, I'm good. I slept well and have *no* regrets. If I had to relive that situation da *only* thing I'd do differently is leave Man at da house. If I'm in a jam and my life's at stake, I'm on demon time no ifs, ands, or buts about it. We live in a concrete jungle. It's kill to survive, I'm gonna survive e'rytime, I'm not gone be nobody pack, straight up."

Knock-Knock shook L's hand and hugged him. "Straight up. On another and more important note, tho. You know Jed's got dem cameras inside and out, so this shooting was recorded. 12 undoubtedly got you and Man's faces on camera. That being said, arrests are inevitable, it's only a question of when you'll get booked. Da word is buddy had a pipe on him, but it's all speculation until there's some valid confirmation. At any rate, that puts you in a better position, defense-wise. I got 50k put up, and Cass is a *certified* fraud queen. Nobody in Indiana or da 'Raq can touch her. We can crack some cards and get enough paper to hire Kristin Long, the best high-powered criminal defense attorney in da City. She should be able to break dis case down and beat it or get you sumn' decent. I'ma shoot to her office and see what she talmbout." Knock-Knock wasn't letting his brother go down with a fight. "In terms of your arrest, you got two options… stay on da run til they catch you, or do what I believe the lawyer gone say, which is turn yourself in. I'm gonna leave that decision up to you. Regardless of how it pan out, I'm gonna make sure you go in with at least five bands to make sho you good while you on da deck. What's yo thoughts?"

"I trust yo judgment bro, so whatever you tell me is best is what I'm standing on. Turning myself in tho make me feel like a *bitch*, straight up. But if that's what it come down to, so be it. If I have to hit da joint tho, on gang I'm looking to get blessed by da Mob."

***

Man was petrified at school. When Diamond dropped him off earlier, he was tempted to skip the whole day, but he knew by lunchtime the school would send Diamond an email notifying her of his absences and she'd be blowing his cellphone up. He reluctantly went to his classes but was a nervous wreck all the while. He struggled to keep himself together. Man intentionally distanced himself from everyone while trying to appear normal.

Every second of the day, Man kept thinking that he'd be summoned to the school's front office and a couple of police officers would be there to arrest him. He would be completely embarrassed. Today was Man's worst school day ever. In between classes, when people tried to stop and talk to him as normally done, he'd nonchalantly say "sup, I gotta take care of sumn"; or, "'alright now'" and keep walking towards his next class.

He made it through all of his classes without incident and was headed to the gym locker room to change clothes for football practice. Man's heartbeat was still erratic as it had been since Saturday. His stomach was turning, and he wanted to duck football practice, but his loyalty and commitment to his goal wouldn't let him waver, even slightly.

***

Detectives Simmons and Goodman reviewed Jed's video footage together several times. The video showed the two juvenile faces clearly, and the Detectives now had a vivid idea of what transpired in the store that resulted in the murder of McCarren. Simmons paused the video in different locations to extract screenshots of Man and L's faces, enlarging them before printing each for identification. Each detective took one suspect's picture and began a computer search for an affirmative identity of Man and L. Because neither of the juveniles had a criminal record, the Detectives' search came up empty.

After the investigation came to a halt with the CPD criminal files, Simmons had an idea. "Let's try DMV's records then," he said to himself. He began sifting through online photographs of African American males aged 15-25 because he didn't know how old either suspect was. He cautiously looked at one picture at a time while simultaneously taking sips of his hot coffee.

After hours of sifting through tons of criminal and DMV photographs, the investigation warmed up when he got a hit on the shooter—Lamont Stewart. "*Gotcha!*" Simmons blurted excitedly. He sat his coffee mug down on his desk and gazed at the enlarged color photo of L on his computer screen. Simmons immediately clicked the print button on his computer using his mouse, as if L's picture was going to self-destruct and vanish from the system. The printer started behind him. Goodman arose from his computer and rushed to the printer to see the now-identified suspect for himself.

"This is our shooter?" Goodman asked surprisingly as he looked over L's printed ID picture.

"Yep!" Simmons exclaimed happily. "Lamont Stewart, who lives on S. Peoria, two blocks west from the store *and* that's the direction both suspects came from and ran towards when leaving. Now we need to figure out who's his partner is so we can book both of them for murder."

"Good job Simms. You wanna work on my guy while I see what additional information I can find out on your guy here?"

"Sure, I'm on a roll, why not?"

Fifteen minutes later, "*Bingo!*" Simmons shouted, staring at his computer monitor at Man's picture like he was possessed. "Malik Williams lives on S. Sangamon, three blocks west of the store. I bet they're childhood friends. They only lived one block apart and they're the same age." Simmons stared at his computer monitor looking at Man's ID picture and the screenshots of him side-by-side comparing every detail just as he did L, all of Man's description matched except his weight. This puzzled Simmons a bit, but he discarded the discrepancy.

Simmons looked up the address listed on Man's ID card just as he'd done with L, to determine if the residence was owned or rented. He gained further information on Man. He was living with his mother, named Diamond Williams. Simmons felt they were on the right track.

"Hey Goodman, anything else on Stewart?"

"Yeah, sounds like he lives with his parents on Peoria and the house is being rented. I'm currently on hold with an admin at Julian High School while they're checking their records if he's one of their students."

Simmons returned with yet another idea while his partner was on hold. Quickly, he Googled both youths' names. Nothing came up on L, but Man was a different story. To his surprise, a plethora of information was available. Everything about his athletic endeavors. He began sifting through the wealth of information.

Goodman broke Simmons' trance. "Simm, the kid's a student at Julian, and he hasn't shown up for any of his classes today."

"Yeah, I know," Simmons said very low while still fixated on his computer monitor. "So is Williams. He's their football star. You still on the phone with them?"

"No. You want me to call back, I gotta direct line."

"No. No, don't call back. Let's just pay a visit back to Roseland and see what we can get."

15

The Detectives pulled up to Julian based on Simmons' hunch that Man would be at football practice considering his apparent devotion to the sport. The Detectives walked into Julian's front office, introduced themselves to the Receptionist, and showed their CPD badges before handing her Man's enlarged ID picture. "Can you tell us if this young man was present for his classes today?" Goodman led the conversation.

Tiffany, the Receptionist that Goodman had spoken with earlier, accepted the picture and looked over and spotted Man's government name on the ID picture and inquired, "Is this the student's name up top?"

Both detectives replied in sync, "Yes."

Within a few seconds of the detectives' confirmation, Tiffany had Man's student profile on her computer monitor. "Mr. Williams reported to each of his classes today officers."

"Thank you, ma'am," Goodman said.

"One last thing, if I may," Simmons said in the friendliest voice he could conjure as if he was out to win cop of the year despite having nefarious intentions to bury two more African American youths in the penal system.

"Sure, go ahead."

"Can you give us directions to your gym football field, please?"

After receiving the requested directions, Simmons thanked her again. The Detectives left the office the same way they entered.

Once outside, Simmons turned to his partner. "You want the gym or field?"

"I'll take the gym; you take the field."

After Goodman took a picture with his cellphone of Man's ID, the Detectives split up and went their separate ways.

Detective Goodman entered the quiet, empty gym. It was just as he suspected it would be. Scanning his surroundings, he found the boys' locker room, entered it, and started searching. He noticed the lockers were secured with individual locks. He hoped this was a good sign that someone was in there so that he could locate Man's locker and search it for incriminating evidence. Goodman paced through the locker room with caution toward what appeared to be a coach's office. He grabbed the office door handle and tried turning it either way. It was locked. "Damnit." After releasing the locked door handle, he resumed moving and peering around the locker room. He heard several noises in the distance, then a sports whistle blew.

  Goodman followed the sounds until he reached a door, where the sounds grew louder and closer. He exited through the door, which introduced him to the Jaguars' football field where practice was being held. While Simmons approached an adult who seemed to have some coaching authority, he shifted his focus to the play in motion. He watched a stocky youngster run the ball so smoothly and swiftly that he prayed it wasn't Man, and if it was, that he wouldn't run because he or his partner would catch him if he did.

Simmons approached an African-American man on the sideline and casually introduced himself as a homicide detective. Simmons extended his right to the gentleman. The tall, stocky, dark-skinned man peered down at Simmons and reluctantly shook his hand. "Assistant Coach Horne, Michael Horne. What can I do for you, Detective?"

"You have a star running back, Malik Williams, playing for you. Is he here, Coach?"

"Yeah, he's here. What seems to be the problem, Detective? Did he have a death in the family or something?"

"He's a person of interest in a murder investigation, Coach, and I have a few questions for him."

"Murder?! Malik hasn't killed anybody. He doesn't have that in him. All he does is play sports and go to school. He's not caught up in that other stuff these youngsters are, I *assure* you of that. Also, he's a minor, so you won't be asking him any questions without the presence of his mother or a lawyer. We know our rights around here."

"Okay. Can you point him out for me, Coach?"

"That's him wearing the number 10 jersey, talking to our head coach."

"Thanks for your cooperation, Coach."

At that very moment, Goodman was walking up to his partner. The two of them began walking towards Man and Coach Skinner.

Man felt eerie and began looking around. He spotted the Detectives immediately—two white men in cheap suits about to disrupt practice. They definitely weren't recruiters.

"Damnit," Man said while trying to keep cool. His first thought was to run for his life, but he again knew he had nowhere to run to, so he stood there, a nervous wreck. His nightmare was now becoming a reality. They somehow uncovered his identity. Somebody snitched. Either Mr. Jed or L. How else could they find him so fast without a record? Man was in his head, and heavy. With his heart racing and full of adrenaline, his hands were trembling. His hearing was no longer operational and his legs were ready to give out.

When the Detectives reached the Coach and Malik, they introduced themselves to both, as Simmons did with Coach Horne. Simmons got straight to his point. "Malik Williams? We have some questions we'd like to ask you down at the station."

Man stood in complete silence from his disappointment and heartache. Coach Skinner put his hand on Man's shoulder. "Malik, you're a minor. Don't answer *any* questions without your mom or a lawyer present." Coach Skinner's touch caused him to snap out of his daze. He wasted no time telling both detectives he wanted a lawyer to be present, which effectively prevented the Detectives from asking him questions.

With all this resistance and rights being asserted by the coaches and Man, Simmons became visibly upset and did what they came for. "Very well, you'll get your lawyer, and in that case, Malik Williams, you're under arrest for the murder of Christopher McCarren. Turn around and place your hands behind your back,"

Simmons said, grabbing Man's right hand and bending it upward to gain control to prevent him from running.

A tear rolled down Man's cheek. He was experiencing the worst humiliation in his life thus far – being arrested in front of his teammates and coaches for a crime he had absolutely nothing to do with.

All his teammates stopped practice and stared in disheartening disbelief. It took only one player to yell out, "Stay down Gang, keep it solid! We love you, bro!" Before the entire team began shouting over each other.

Once the Detectives got Man in the car and drove off, the Detectives looked at each other cheerfully, then Simmons looked in his rear-view mirror at Man. "Malik, I read many articles about you and watched several of your highlights. I know that you've got *at least* 4 confirmed offers from D-1 schools. I also know you didn't kill anyone. Give us Lamont, the real shooter, and you can sleep in your own bed tonight. Or you can 'stay down' like your boys said and I'll personally see to it that your face is plastered all over WGN news for a murder arrest and you can kiss those D-1's and college football goodbye. You got until we get to the jail to think about it."

Goodman chimed in, "Yeah, Malik man, you seem like a good kid. You got a lot going on. No need to sacrifice everything because your buddy did something stupid. Do the right thing and get back to your life and family. Use your talent to get your family out of Chicago."

16

After Diamond's shift ended, she clocked out and began walking to her car. Her same routine for the last several years. After getting inside her Honda Accord and starting the engine, she ensured her car doors were locked, then turned on her cellphone. Several notifications from Coach Skinner and Horne flooded her phone about Man. Two voicemails and four text messages. She didn't know definitively who the voicemails were from, so she went straight to her texts.

"Diamond, please call me or come to the field *ASAP*. CPDs here wanting to question Man."

The second message was time-stamped two minutes later.

"They just arrested Man and are escorting him off. I don't know what the charges are."

Diamond then went to Coach Skinner's texts, hoping to gain some information before freaking out. His first message was a short video of the Detectives walking with a handcuffed Man in between them, each detective holding Man's arms.

"NOOOOOO! MY BABYYYYY!!!" Diamond screamed like she watched Man get murdered, and then she broke down bawling, forming puddles on her clothes. Diamond's scream was so loud that a couple of passers heading into Jewels heard the shriek.

In literal seconds, Diamond's world, her life, had been destroyed. Everything she worked hard for. Everything she put her blood, sweat, and tears into had proven to be *a failure* because this is exactly what she worked hard to avoid. These thoughts and even more crossed her mind in the minutes she sat in the parking lot trying to cry away this pain. A nightmare. No warning, welcome, or reasoning.

"I *knew* it! I *knew* something was wrong! *Dammit*, Man, *why* didn't you talk to me? I gave you multiple opportunities to tell me what was wrong!" Diamond shouted out of frustration, like he was sitting in her passenger seat. Diamond lifted her tear-soaked cellphone, unlocked it again, and then read her final unread message from Coach Skinner.

"Diamond, I regret to inform you, the Detectives arrested Man while I was talking to him, for the murder of 'Christopher McCarren'. This name doesn't ring a bell, and I think there may be some kind of mix-up given my confidence Man isn't in the streets. At any rate, I told the Detectives in front of Man they couldn't question him without you, a guardian, or an attorney present due to him being a minor. Man also told them in front of me he wanted a lawyer so they shouldn't question him, but it's CPD. I'm truly sorry to have to tell you this, and if there's anything I can do for you, or Man please don't hesitate to let me know. Feel free to contact me at any time."

When Diamond reached the part of Coach Skinner's message concerning Man being charged with murder, she cried even harder knowing the seriousness of the allegations, and she paused there for several minutes before reading the remainder of the message.

Shattered, Diamond put the car in drive and left the parking lot to go home and sob privately.

***

The unmarked Crown Victoria transporting the Detectives and Man reached the Juvenile Justice Center (JJC) in St. Charles, Illinois, where juveniles from ages ten through sixteen are housed pending delinquent or criminal charges. Detective Simmons eased into the parking spot as Detective Goodman slowly turned down the music and looked over his left shoulder at Man cuffed in the back seat.

"Man, we're at your new home unless you wanna talk to us. Have you had a change of heart?" Detective Goodman cynically said.

Man looked out the passenger back window with a straight face taking in as much of the view as he could because he knew it'd be an unknown amount of time before he would see it again.

The silence that lingered in the car was broken by Detective Simmons' frustration. "Hey! Man! Don't ignore my partner. Whatcha gonna do? With or without you, we're gonna bury your buddy Lamont. This is a matter of whether you want to save yourself or go down with him."

Now upset with the Detectives' attempt to bully and frighten him more than he was already frightened, Man looked at them and whispered, "If I cooperate, how soon will I be released?"

Both Detectives felt a rush of bliss. Man was taking the bait to help them capture L so they could send him and Man both to prison for the longest possible term, unbeknownst to him.

"Immediately," they excitedly said in sync.

Man dropped his head, his chin rested on his chest as he painfully said, "Aight, I'll help y'all."

The Detectives wanted to celebrate right then, but they kept their cool despite their faces noticeably lighting up like the oversized, decorated downtown Chicago Christmas tree. Simmons scrambled to pull out his small, digital voice recorder to record Man's 'voluntary' statement. When he pushed the record button, he began recording himself first. "This is Detective Raymond Simmons and I have my partner

Detective Joey Goodman present with me. We are sitting in our assigned, unmarked detective vehicle. We have in custody our murder suspect Malik Williams, who en route to JJC to be booked for murder, Mr. Williams voluntarily decided he wanted to cooperate with our investigation by rescinding his imposition of the right to counsel. Mr. Williams, your cooperation is being recorded and you're now free to speak," he said as he held the digital voice recorder toward the back seat.

Simmons stared at Man, eagerly waiting for him to give whatever details he was going to share to help their case. Man slowly lifted his head and took a deep breath, knowing what he was about to do would give everyone something to talk about for quite some time.

Man looked at both detectives in their eyes and muttered, "I'll help y'all." Then even louder, he said, "I'll help y'all understand what I already said, I WANT A LAWYER! Now take me to my cell and quit playing with me!" he said matter of factly.

Detective Simmons' face went from gleeful to flush red in an instant from vexation. He snatched his digital voice recorder back, stopping the recording. He looked at Man and sternly said "Okay, tough guy, have it your way. Malik Williams will be headline talk tomorrow morning, but it won't be for any sports accomplishments."

The Detectives exited the vehicle and Goodman removed Man from the backseat behind him, knowing that his partner was utterly flustered and wasn't ideal for handling Man currently. They took Man into JJC and booked him.

***

Diamond arrived home still crying, but no longer sobbing. She went in her room and allowed herself to cry a bit more then collected herself as best she could so that she could begin getting information on Man. First, she called Coach Skinner to get as much information as possible from him. After concluding her twenty-minute call with the Coach, Diamond had enough information to contact the arresting Detectives to get more detailed information on Man's situation.

Diamond dialed Detective Simmons' direct line and got his voicemail due to it being after hours. She reluctantly left him a message knowing her call wouldn't be returned until the following day. She then hung up and called CPD's general number to get information on Man's housing; visiting times/days; and his court date. From her second phone call, Diamond made progress: she had his address; booking number; visiting schedule; and his pending court date.

Diamond sent her boss a text requesting to get Wednesday off so that she could attend Man's court date and see what's going on with her son. Given Diamond was a store manager, and never took sick days from work, her boss was more than willing to accommodate her and told her to take Wednesday through Friday off to give herself some time to process and regroup.

<u>Tuesday, September 26, 2023</u>

"Aight, bet. Good lookin', love," Knock-Knock said, as he ended his brief phone call.

"Man got popped for murder today. Twelve snatched him up from practice. He lawyered up, so it sounds like he gone keep it solid," Knock-Knock told L as they rode to their next destination.

Just as Knock-Knock finished his statement, L pounded his fist into the passenger door. "Damn! I jagged off bro future." He dropped his head in genuine disappointment.

"In a sense, you're right and in another you're wrong. Did you force him to go to the sto' with you?" Knock-Knock countered.

"Naw," L answered sadly. "But if I hadn't told him to slide up there with me in the first place, he would've never went. He was at da crib coolin' after his game. *I* wanted to go to Jed's to get sumn' to eat, and no cap we could've ate at his house. His OG keep food fo his ass. I didn't wanna deal with Diamond cuz I know she low-key don't like me."

Trying to provide his little brother some comfort, Knock-Knock said, "I hear you L, but you gotta remember, Man could've easily told you he was straight and not went. Both of y'all know where y'all at and what be happening throughout da City in da hood. It ain't no secret to either of y'all. How many studs got turnt into a pack fallin' off inna sto in Chicago?"

"Damn bro! Dis whole situation is bogish, straight up."

"You right, lil bro, but it is what it is. Ain't no turning back now." Knock-Knock said, while keeping his eyes on the road.

The brothers rode in silence, having their thoughts while Fly Skinz's 'Roseland's Very Best' pumped out of the Q60's speakers. L broke the silence. "KK take me back to da City. I'ma turn myself in. I can't let bro take da hit like that."

Shocked, Knock-Knock turned the music down a little and looked at L for a few. "You *sho* that's what you wanna do, or you on an emotional trip right now?"

"Yeah, Man gotta life and future ahead of 'em. He ain't do nun and ain't have nun to do wit dat shit. That's bro and I can't see him takin' da fall fo what I did. I'll turn myself in and ride da bid. Hopefully, they'll cut bro loose and he can get back to school."

Knock-Knock took a deep breath, hearing the authenticity in L's voice. He knew with certainty that his days with his brother were now numbered. It happened sooner than he had expected. He wanted to talk L out of his decision, but he knew it was the right thing to do and he'd never heard that level of sincerity from his little brother about anything before. He knew L would be forced to do some growing up that he may not otherwise do in the streets. "Aight, check it out. Let's bust these last cards and I'll have more than enough to hire your lawyer, send you off with some paper, and not be broke. Tomorrow I'll contact the lawyer and see what she on. If she talking right, we'll arrange for you to turn yourself in through her."

"Aight," L replied, fearing the unknown.

17

<u>Wednesday, September 27, 2023</u>

Due to the severity of Man's charges, and intending to hold someone responsible for the apparent gang-related murder, the assistant state attorney successfully sought a juvenile release denial against Man and got the case transferred to adult court, which led to Man being immediately moved to the Cook County jail.

Diamond came to Man's court date by herself. Seeing her son herded into court like an animal broke her spirit. She sat silently on the side of the defense. When Man came into the courtroom, he made eye contact with Diamond; she didn't have to say a word, her look said everything. Man, dropped his head in shame.

A representative from the public defender's office came over to talk with Man briefly and collect some information before focusing on the court proceeding. His attorney, whom Man didn't catch the name of, did minimal in countering the assistant state attorney's efforts to have Man's juvenile release denied, and his case transferred to adult court.

After Man's court hearing, Diamond waited in the court's corridor for Man's helpless attorney to step out of the courtroom. The lawyer, an older Caucasian man, stepped into the corridor hurriedly while Diamond sat on a bench tightly clutching her purse. The instant she saw him, Diamond stood up. "Excuse me. *Excuse me, sir.*"

Peter Hatcher turned toward the soft-spoken voice. "I'm sorry. Are you calling me?"

"I certainly am! Can I have a few moments of your time, please?" urged Diamond.

"I have somewhere to be now. Can you make it quick?" the elder stated.

"Sure. I'll make it *real* quick," Diamond sliced at him. "My name is Diamond Williams. I'm the mother of Malik Williams."

"I'm sorry, who?" Hatcher stuttered.

"*Malik Williams*, the young man you were just talking to and representing in court who you did absolutely nothing for. Listen to me, my son is not another animal you'll be herding to the penitentiary or swapping out for a more favorable client. Please, give me your card so that his private counsel can contact you and have you relieved of your duty *immediately*."

Mr. Hatcher handed Diamond his card. "Are we finished here, Ms. Williams? I must leave now."

"*For now*," Diamond said with serious disdain.

After leaving the courthouse, Diamond went into survivor mode and researched the best criminal defense attorneys in Cook County. She narrowed her list down to five attorneys, and after consulting with three of the five, Diamond settled on a big dog, Mark Siroka, to represent Man. Once meeting with Siroka, Diamond was advised he wanted a fifty thousand dollar retainer for Man's case, given the severity of the charges. His billable hours were four hundred dollars an hour. Half of the retainer was required for Siroka to accept the case, the other half would be due just before trial or the taking of a plea.

Diamond left Siroka's office and went home. She immediately went to her bedroom, turned the light on in her deep walk-in closet, and moved what appeared to be a pile of miscellaneous junk around to uncover the small, heavy safe she previously had bolted to the floor in the back of her closet. She opened the safe and pulled out five stacks of banded ten thousand dollars. Realizing she would need money orders she placed the money back in the safe, and contacted her broker to advise him that she needed to sell fifty thousand dollars worth of her investments so that she could hire an attorney for her son. The broker advised her that her funds should be available within forty-eight hours.

After handling business with her broker, Diamond again cried herself to sleep, heartbroken over her son's situation.

This was the first time she'd been at home without him in his seventeen years of living, unless he spent the night with his grandparents or a friend or attended one of his sports functions.

Thursday, September 28, 2023

The morning sun had risen upon Chicago. Diamond's parents were having breakfast together, and a story from WGN News had come on their TV.

"We're reporting to update you on the story of seventeen-year-old Malik Williams, whom most of us know from the sports segment as a promising football star. Williams was recently charged for his alleged participation in a gang-related murder. We don't know the extent of his involvement, but we do know that Williams, the Percy L. Julian High School star running back, was arrested on September 25th. Originally, Williams was charged as a minor, but yesterday our crew was present in court when the assistant state attorney successfully moved to charge Williams as an adult. This decision will lead to Williams suffering a stiffer penalty if convicted of the charged crimes. We will continue to follow this unfortunate story and keep you updated on any new developments."

"What the hell?" Diamond's father, Horace exclaimed.

Diamond's mother, Carrie, whispered in an utterly shocked tone, "Oh my God!"

It wasn't long before Diamond was awakened by her mother's phone calls and text messages. When she saw it was her mother calling, Diamond put her phone on silent and cried. Seeing Carrie's messages broke Diamond's heart more, so she laid back down and tried her hardest to melt into her mattress. She thought today would be better, and she'd be able to get up and do her daily activities, but her reality was simply too much for her to face.

Diamond was sound asleep when Carrie arrived at her house to check on her daughter. After Diamond failed to answer Carrie's two separate rounds of knocking, she pulled out her spare key and let herself in. "*Diamond! Diamond! Diamond,* baby!" The complete silence throughout the house spooked Carrie, so she reached into her purse and pulled out her cellphone in the event she needed to call 911. Carrie arrived at Diamond's bedroom and found her sound asleep.

Carrie walked over to Diamond's bed and sat on the edge. She looked around, absorbing the scene – an open box of Puff's Lotion Plus facial tissues on the nightstand sitting beside Diamond's bed while several used tissues were scattered across the floor next to the bed. Carrie's heart broke, but she knew she had to be strong for her daughter. Carrie gently caressed Diamond's back and added soft, motherly taps as if she were still a child. "Diamond, wake up, baby. C'mon, wake up sweetie," Carrie continued in her sweet, motherly voice.

Diamond groggily woke up, slowly processing her surroundings, and not really recalling what transpired that led her to sleep. Her eyes eventually set upon Carrie, and she looked at her mother with a look of total brokenness, then began sobbing profusely. Carrie hugged Diamond tightly, wrapping her hand around the back of Diamond's head, and began gently patting. "Aww baby, don't cry, it's okay. Tell Mama what's going on." After nearly fifteen minutes of bawling, Diamond sat up and blew all the collected snot from her nose into several tissues, then patted her eyes and face dry with a couple of fresh tissues.

Diamond told Carrie everything she knew about Man's arrest and told her that she was waiting to talk to or see Man to find out as much as she could without compromising his case. She also shared with Carrie that she's already found a private attorney for Man and has cashed out some of her investments to cover the cost. Carrie assured Diamond that she and Horace would do whatever they could to support Man throughout this process.

<u>Friday, September 29, 2023</u>

When Diamond awoke in the late morning, she went to have a cigarette at her kitchen window as she normally did after eating some breakfast and sipping on a cup of coffee. An email notification alerted her cellphone, but she finished up her Kool cigarette before checking the notification. She picked up her cellphone, unlocked it, and pulled down the status bar to see the preview of the notification. To her surprise and somewhat happiness, it was an email from Blackwell Investments, LLC. Diamond clicked on the notification, which transferred her to the email. It was short and direct.

Dear Ms. Williams, please be advised that your requested assets have been sold and your funds are now available. Please contact me at your earliest convenience to arrange your receipt of the funds.

Corrine Blackwell

Diamond called Corrine immediately and arranged for an electronic transfer of the funds to her bank account. Then she called Siroka, the attorney she intended to hire for Man to make arrangements to have the money electronically transferred into his account immediately after it reached her checking account.

Siroka told Diamond he'd have his receptionist send her the retainer agreement as soon as possible. While Diamond and Siroka were on their call, the money arrived in her account. "*Please*, provide me with your banking information so that I can send your money, Mark. I don't wanna wait for your receptionist or the contract. You and I know what the money is for and I'm sure your contract will specify all the details, so let me send you this money so that you're locked in with my son."

Mark provided Diamond his bank routing number and moments later, he received a notification that fifty thousand dollars had been received. He was caught completely off-guard. "Ms. Williams, I received the *total* amount from you. I wasn't requiring, nor expecting the full retainer."

"I'm aware of what your expectations were. However, this is my son's life, my only child. I don't play about him. I paid you in full so you can not only get started immediately, but also so you know how serious I am about my son getting the best representation. I need you to do nothing less than your absolute best for Malik. I have fulfilled my obligation to you. Now fulfill yours to us," Diamond said matter-of-factly.

"Diamond, I understand your position and concern, and again, I'm sorry for your son's situation. You will have the full support of my office in Malik's representation, I assure you. Please sign the retainer agreement and return it at your leisure. I will file an attorney of record motion with the court today and contact the assistant public defender on Malik's case to notify him you've hired me to take over the case. Have a pleasant day and I'll be in touch soon."

Unbeknownst to Diamond, a couple of hours after she hired Siroka, Man was transferred to Cook County jail. After his arrival and processing into the jail, Man was sent to Division 5, the jail's youth 'gladiator school'. All of Chicago's incarcerated youth, aged 16-21, who hadn't completed high school, were housed here. D-5 as it was commonly known had earned the title 'gladiator school' because of the level of violence that occurred in this respective unit, it was filled with pure testosterone with no drive other than to show an individual's ability to be the toughest savage in the City. Despite it being said on paper, attending school is mandatory for its inmates. It was the *last* thing on the majority's mind as Man quickly learned.

***

Once he arrived at his assigned cell in D-5, Man was met at the threshold by another young man who already occupied the cell. He opened the door the instant he heard it unlock to confront his tentative celly. He stood bare chested in the doorway with his t-shirt tied around his deadlocked head. "What's up folks, I'm

Money from da Low End. Where you from, Gang?" he asked.

Man instantly froze. He had a flashback hearing Money's introduction, and he missed everything said after, *what's up, folks?* Because the last time he heard those exact words, loud gunshots followed. Momentarily, Man was back in Jed's that Saturday all over again. He was traumatized. When Man came back to his senses, he replied, "What's good, bro?" He tried to move to enter the cell, but Money hadn't budged.

"Where you from, Gang?" Money repeated.

"I'm from Roseland. I ain't plugged," Man replied, stuttering, and still trying to recover from his flashback.

"Aight, just making sho you wasn't a opp. 12 be playing games, bro," Money said as he moved out of Man's way.

Man entered the cell, sat his belongings down, and began cleaning the top bunk area to make it comfortable for himself while having small talk with Money about who each other knew from their respective hoods to verify their identities with one another in adherence to the hood protocols. During their exchange, Money explained to Man that fights are the norm in the unit and that he was going to be tested since he was a 'neutron' meaning he was not affiliated with any gangs and some would see him as easy prey.

18

<u>Saturday, September 30, 2023</u>

Man was awakened by knocks to the bottom of the upper bunk. "Man... Man, they gone be runnin' chow in a minute, Gang."

Man leaned up on his elbow and saw Money dressed and ready like he'd been up for a while. Man stretched his body and sat upright on his hardened bed comprising a badly battered cot resting on a slab of lifeless steel, then hopped off his bunk to the floor to put on his shoes, wash his face, and brush his teeth.

After brushing his teeth to slay his morning dragon breath, Man told Money, "Good looking on waking me up, bro, I appreciate it."

"It's good, Gang." Money then laced Man up on the release program. "When they crack the doors, don't step out da room for your tray until you hear the worker say, 'everyone else.'"

In a confused state, Man asked, "Why's that?"

"There's control movement in here, Joe, like da joint. When 12 pop da doors, one of da guys will step out and make da call for alla da folks to step out for dey trays, then da brothers will make the call, then the worker will call for the neutrons. If anyone breaks either Mob's chain, it's gone be ugly."

"Aw okay, bet."

The breakfast release ran exactly how Money said, and everyone respected the release. When the call was made for the neutrons, Man stepped out of the cell and put his back against the wall on the tier, letting others pass him by so he would be last and see who was in the unit he may know. He joined the line after he believed everyone had exited their cells. When he reached the worker to receive his breakfast tray, he was addressed by the worker. "Wassup Gang, where you from?"

"Roseland," Man said sternly as his intuition alerted him because of his observance of the worker not grabbing a tray for him as he'd done for everyone before him.

"Smooth. I'm Beast from Gary, fin ball. Aye, we short trays bruh, come back at tray return and I'ma see if 12 can get you one," the worker said.

"W'sup with those few trays right there?" Man asked as he slightly jerked his head up towards the trays behind Beast.

"Those for me and da guys bro, I'll get at…"

Beast's reply was curtailed with no warning or hesitation when Man hit him with a quick jab and hook to the jawline, then a solid left hook to the liver. Knocking over the trays they were just discussing, Beast stumbled backward. Beast and the trays both fell to the floor. Man, immediately stood over Beast to finish him but told him, "Check it out Beast, I ain't plugged and I ain't for *nun* either. Make this your first and last time you or your guys try ta take *anything* from me. I ain't accepting no l's in here, straight up!"

Man returned to his cell visibly upset. In less than twenty-four hours, he was being tried, and he was returning to his cell empty-handed. However, he knew that he'd just kept his dignity and sent a clear message to all onlookers. Man wasn't about to be bullied.

<u>Wednesday, October 4, 2023</u>

A few days after Man reached the county jail, L made arrangements through Knock-Knock and his private counsel, Kristin, to surrender peacefully by turning himself in to CPD. After his surrender, L was processed into JJC just as Man had been. However, L remained in JJC longer than Man because Kristin was adamant in opposing the assistant state attorney's efforts to have L transferred to adult court. Unfortunately, Kristin would lose the fight and L also was transferred to Cook County jail.

While L was in JJC, Man was mentally struggling with his new and foreign living conditions. He had his first phone calls and visit with Diamond while he was in the county jail, Man told her as much as he could about the case on a visit without implicating himself or L. Diamond told Man about his private counsel and that she put $500 on his books for him to purchase his necessities.

Nearly three months after turning himself in, L was transferred to the county jail and would land in D-5 with Man. After getting settled into his cell, L learned from his celly that Man was in the same unit as him and that he'd already put down a few demonstrations for the unit's occupants. L put together a 'kite' for Man and had the worker Beast drop the kite off to him.

Upon receiving the kite, Man opened it and began reading.

Man, what's the deal, Gang. I just pulled up and I'm downstairs in room 5 (ironically).

Anyway, when I heard you got popped, I immediately planned to turn myself in to get dis bid off ya. Brother, I'm truly sorry for getting you caught up in my stuff. Every day I wish we would've just stayed at yo crib, we'd never be in this jam. I hope that you'll find it in yo heart to forgive me for jaggin' off your life and plans. KK got me a lawyer. I'm gonna get at her about a decent deal so I can get you cut loose, and you can get back to yo OG and doing yo school stuff. When you done reading this kite, be sure to rip it up and flush it so 12 don't get it and pull up on me when you can, bro. Love! L

After reading the kite, Man did exactly as instructed and hopped back on his bunk and stared at the ceiling in deep thought.

Evening dayroom came around. Man and L were once again in the same place. This reality was uneasy for Man. The last time he and L were together like this, his life as he then knew it had been catapulted into a barrage of chaos. Gunshots, burnt gunpowder, a dead man, and arrested for murder.

This was an awkward moment for L because he knew his actions caused everything that had transpired in both of their lives since that Saturday in Jed's. L didn't regret the murder, not even a little bit, yet the fact that *his* actions destroyed his best friend's life haunted him heavily, and at the very least, he wanted to make *that* right.

"Wassup Gang?" L said to Man as they shook hands and embraced.

"It ain't nun. What you on, bro?"

"Let's hit that corner to keep these studs out da bidness, Gang," stated L as he led Man to an empty corner in the dayroom. They turned their backs to the wall as L began, "Man, bro, for real for real Gang, my fault fa getting' you caught up in dis. If I knew dis was gone happen, I would've stayed coolin' on da porch with you, straight up. Ion really know whatchu feelin bro, but my word, I'm willing to do whatever it takes to get da case off you and get you back to yo family and your team so you can pursue yo dreams. You can have yo lawyer get at me or whatever. "

"I appreciate it bro, but ion think there's much you can do to make me whole at dis point. 12 blasted my face all over da news like I was some kinda of captured terrorist cuz I wouldn't get down on you, so college is *over*, straight up. At least as far as a scholarship is concerned. Once this case is over, I gotta go back to da drawing board to figure out my life. So, fa now, let's just focus on getting da best outcome from dis case cuz I see ain't nobody but you tryna or gonna do the right thing. My OG got me a lawyer too. I had some goofy ass PD, and she wasn't havin it."

"They put you on da *news?!*"

"Yep. I didn't see it. My OG told me my grandparents saw it tho, and they've been covering da story daily since I got popped. Dirty ass pig carried out his promise, I guess."

L sighed and dropped his head just as he did when he learned Man was arrested. "They bogish as hell, Gang. Damn. It was on video, they *know* you ain't do nun."

"They got the video. That's how they got our identities. Those two pigs couldn't give a damn about da video. All they cared about was arresting our black asses to send us to da joint."

"I'm bouta hit the jugg, you need anything bro?"

"Naw, I'm straight Joe. My OG put some money on my books. How you get popped anyway?"

"I told you, I turned myself in G."

"Turned yourself *in*???? You was serious?"

"Yeah. Soon as KK told me you got popped, I told 'em I was turning myself in, I couldn't let you take da fall for my rap."

"Fa sho. I gotta hop on da phone and shower bro, we'll rap tomorrow or sumn."

"Aight, bet. I heard you been getting wild in here Gang, what you on?"

"I ain't on nun bro, these studs think I'ma fold cuz I'ma neutron. I ain't goin for it, I'm standin on bidness e'ry time they wanna tweak with me. Straight up."

"I can dig it. I already told da guys you my brotha, so you good wit da fin til you leave."

"L, I ain't doin no aid and assist bro. I'm standin on my own 10, no bap."

"Naw, it ain't even like that bro, you ain't under nothing but my brotherhood. I know how you move."

"Bet. I gotta make some calls shordy. I'll get up wit you tomorrow. Love bro."

"Aight. Love!"

19

After a few months of sitting in the county jail and making several court appearances, Man's attorney, Mark, was able to get him a deal serving 80% of three years with one year of time served. Man would serve roughly 16 additional months of incarceration for accessory to murder. After consulting with Diamond and L, Man took the deal so he could get to the next page of his life and get the heck out of the jail.

Man wasn't too pleased with his deal. He was pleading guilty for something he truly had *nothing* to do with. Although he would not be serving much time, and it was only a fraction of the maximum sentence he could get by losing at trial, it was still a portion of his life for simply being at the wrong place at the wrong time. There was nothing fair about it, but the assistant state attorney convinced herself of Man's involvement in the crime by merely looking at L. According to the prosecutor, that glance was a sign from Man for L to shoot McCarren, and *that's* why Man was going to prison, for a *look*. It made him sick to his stomach because it was an imaginary and false narrative that made no sense.

On the flip side, by the time he gets to his destination and establishes his daily routine, or program, as it's called in prison, it'll be time for him to go home. The plea bargain would give Man the opportunity to resolve the case with his dignity intact by not being able to go against L directly or through his attorney on this case.

Monday, November 13, 2023

Judge Leonard K. Karlton's courtroom was packed with Man's supporters at his sentencing. Diamond, Man's grandparents, all of his athletic coaches throughout his life, some teachers from Julian, friends, and family. Bea even showed up, to his surprise. So many spectators filled the Court's audience on both sides and the latecomers were compelled to stand outside in the court's corridor. Most of the attendees got to speak on Man's behalf to support his character.

Seeing Bea made him think about taking her seriously rather than playing with her feelings as he had been doing. She had been nothing but solid with him since they met, even when he didn't have any genuine interest in her because he was focused on his college career and getting his family out of Chicago. The entire time he was in the county jail, Bea sent him letters and pictures. She visited; accepted his calls; and put money on his books, although he didn't need it. All the other young ladies he had dealt with before his arrest had proven unreliable or completely abandoned him.

Judge Karlton heard all the character witness testimony but still sentenced Man to the term of his plea agreement, not a lesser term as his attorney was pushing for. However, he gave Man more pre-sentence credits than what he was entitled, to help him get his actual in-custody time decreased.

When Man returned from his sentencing, L was in the dayroom chilling with one of his guys. This provided the last opportunity for Man and L to have their last heart-to-heart talk for God knows how long. Man stepped into the Unit striving to hold his head high and remain poker-faced, but L knew him better than anyone.

L looked into Man's face and saw a glimmer of melancholy. That look internally crushed L.

He stopped talking and walked up to Man, shook his hand, and hugged him tightly. "What's da word bro, you good?"

Man returned L's genuine hug with a light one. "Honestly, naw, I'm not good bro. I just sacrificed a part of my life for something I had absolutely nothing to do with. My whole life I've avoided pluggin' in with any of y'all to avoid *this* and to get my family outta dis wretched ass city, yet I *still* landed *here*, in jail, with you as my rappy. Because I *looked* at you before *you blew* this stud taco back. This punk ass prosecutor has strung me along with your stupidity under da guise of me somehow being in cahoots wit yo gang activity. Me and my family been stressed out over this case. My family dropped bands they don't have on a lawyer for me cuz of what you did, and now I gotta felony record… for what? Cuz, I made a stupid ass decision to keep dealing wit you when my OG told me repeatedly to stay away from you and other members. So naw, I'm not good at all Joe, straight up."

"Check it out, Chálie. I understand yo frustration and disappointment, and I've apologized to you many times already. I did everything I could to make it right with you, Gang. You know dis. You said it yourself, these white folks are out to hang our black asses, period. Yeah, I'm the reason we are here and I've thought about my actions every day since it happened.

"Have you thought about the *fact* that I saved my and *yo* life by killin' that clown? If I didn't do my duggy we both woulda been in the ground already, both of our families grieving. This Chiraq, da trenches ain't playing out here. It's step or be stepped on, and if I had to do it again, the only thing I'd change is removing you from da equation. But I can't change it, so the next time you think about blaming me for anything, blame me for keepin' yo ass alive brother 'cause I'd rather be here having dis conversation than to be 6 feet under, ya dig?"

A long silence wedged between them until L looked at the ground. "You right, you saved my life, but you ruined it at the same time, so it's a bittersweet feelin', bro. I need some time to digest I'm headed to da joint for nothing," Man said and bounced to his cell.

Tuesday, November 14, 2023

"Aye Gang, 12 said you going to R&C today. You might wanna roll your stuff up so you not rushin' when they call you." Beast informed Man when he was picking up his food.

"Aight, bet. Good lookin' out, Joe." Man took his food back to his cell and shared the news with Money.

"Damn folks, I'ma low-key miss yo stankin' ass, on fo nem. All the time in dis thang, you da best celly I've had so far, straight up. I'm talmbout even da folks ain't been as smooth as you bro, no bap" Money genuinely said.

"It's good bro, I appreciate you Money, and e'rything you showed and told me Joe, fa real. I hope e'rything work out for you on da case bro, straight up. Focus on beatin' dat body and stop trippin' on these studs in here, bro. Get back out there to yo shorty, she gon need you, not da next man, to be there for her. I grew up without my daddy, never even met 'em, it hurts and takes its toll. Y'all don't think about *that* part of da game when y'all sliding on da opps or when dey catch you lacking. When you bring a child in dis world, your life no longer belongs to you. That's my gem to you!"

Man's words resonated with Money. It was clear on his face. "You right bro, you right. I appreciate that. I'm gonna move better for Jordyn. I love my baby." Money then snapped out of that moment and laughed lightly. "Gang, gone wit all dat positivity! But I hear you bro and truly I appreciate your words, but you da same stud dat whooped three people in what, 2 or 3 months?"

"And every one of 'em had it comin' too. Y'all may punk these other neutrons in here, but I ain't going fa nun, straight up. And when I hit da joint, I'm movin' da same way til it's time to go home, on bro." Man firmly said.

Within the hour, their cell door unlocked, and Man knew that was his cue to come out and get ready for his journey to Joliet, Illinois—prison. The duo shook hands and hugged, then said their goodbyes, and Man made his way down the stairs and went to L's cell. Man knocked on the door lightly and called for L. "Bro, you up?" L's celly came to the door and saw Man standing to the side with his belongings then looked at L and told him it was for him.

L jumped down from his top bunk and approached the door "What's da deal, Gang?"

"Bro, I'm gone – R&C. I wanted to let you know I thought about e'rything Joe, and you right, you did what you had to. I honor yo decision bro. I appreciate you saving my life, I don't know if I could or even would've done da same thing if I was in your shoes, so I look at things from yo perspective. I've reluctantly accepted this was my fate, as much as I don't like it, but there's nothing I can do to change any of it. I love you, bro. No hard feelings, and no matter how it turns out I gotchu, on bro."

L's eyes teared up while Man was talking, but he withheld them from dropping. "Man, I appreciate you Gang, no bap. We can't unring a bell Man, what's done is done. Don't cry ova spilt milk Gang, clean it up and keep it movin' bro, straight up. No matter da situation. Bro, you ain't got much left. When you get where you going be smooth, Gang. Fa real, fa real. Don't jag off yo date. I told KK how you movin' in here, he's was surprised, but proud of you. He said if you need or wanna let anybody in da joint know you his lil brother, do so, and you ah be good wherever you at. I love you, bro. We gon get up wit each other again, Gang. Dis ain't da end of it."

"Bet bro. I'm up, love."

"Love, Gang."

20

Friday, January 5, 2024

After sitting in reception for nearly a month and a half, Man was transferred to what he hoped would be his final prison before being released – Centralia Correctional Center. Man landed in a two-man cell at the medium-security prison, in the north cluster. Building 1. His celly was on 'security' for the Black Disciples. His name was Q-Ball, and he was from Lamron. Initially, Man was uneasy about living with Ball considering he was BD and Man was in prison for the murder of a BD; however, what provided him some comfort was where Ball was from. It was very unlikely they knew each other. Man sized Ball up from their first encounter and was confident he could whoop Ball if that's what it came to.

Ball had already served four years and five left, and was almost 10 years older than Man. Ball was real smooth in Man's eyes, yet he monitored him in case he ever heard about his case and wanted to trip. Ball laced Man up on the dos and don'ts in prison and the politics. Man listened intently but had made his mind up in reception that he wanted to just do his time, stay out of everyone's way, and get back home to his family, so he really didn't care about being privy to what was going on in prison especially if it didn't pertain to him.

Man spent the bulk of his time working out on the prison yard to keep his health and physique up while intentionally avoiding people to the best of his ability. He spent time on the prison phones, writing letters, and going on video visits often with Bea to strengthen his relationship with her.

One day, after doing an intense one-and-a-half-hour workout, Man returned to his housing unit seeking to shower and go to his assigned cell to eat and relax. "OG, anyone after you in da shower?" Man asked.

"You got it, young blood. What they call you?"

"Man. They call me Man."

"All right, Man. Let me make my wudu and I'll be out your way in two minutes, young brother. I'm Latif, by the way, a pleasure to meet you," he returned gleefully.

Moments later Latif stepped out of the shower in his shower shoes, boxers, and a T-shirt with his towel hanging on the back of his neck. As he stood on the upper tier drying his feet to put his shoes on, Latif called out, "Man, you up, good brother."

Man looked toward Latif's voice, then headed to the upstairs shower. When he approached Latif, the two locked eyes briefly, and Man nervously uttered, "Good lookin', OG."

Latif paused in the moment for a split-second, processing what he received when he peered into Man's eyes to see his soul as he'd done everyone else he met to determine if he would deal with them, and on what level if so. Latif saw through the frightened fish and softened his approach before responding politely, "No problem, good brother, you're welcome. How are you doing, Man?"

In his humbled, soft monotone voice, Man replied, "I'm good OG. How about you?"

"Alhamdu lillah wa shukr lillah, I'm blessed good brother, thanks for asking. You just drove up?"

"Yeah," Man replied nervously while stepping into the shower area. Man felt vibes from Latif that he'd never experienced with anyone else before. Latif had an aura about himself that he took life seriously, commanded respect and that he wasn't for *none* — especially with staff.

"You from the City?"

"Yeah, Roseland."

"Ah, okay. The Wild Wild, huh? You straight, you need anything, good brother?"

"I'm straight, and good lookin', old school." Man took his shower and went on about his day.

<u>Wednesday, January 24, 2024</u>

Man went to the yard to get some fresh air and work out. He walked a few laps first to stretch his legs a little and get the blood flowing, then he ran a quick ten laps and made his way over to the workout bars. He spotted Latif on the weight pile, working out by himself.

Latif had just completed his third set of twenty-five pull-ups when he locked eyes with Man approaching the pile. Latif extended his right fist in Man's direction as he neared. "As salaamu alaikum, Man."

"What's good, OG?" Man returned as he gave Latif the fist bump. "You getting that money, huh?"

"Yeah, a little bit to keep an old man in decent shape under these circumstances. You kinda chunky under there, good brother. You played ball or something?"

The mentioning of sports sent Man into an instant spiral of memories, anger, and disappointment. Man tried fighting off his feelings and thoughts and answered Latif. "I played football for Julian, was ranked number 2 player in the State."

"Yet you still landed in here, forfeiting your talent to become a slave on the institutional plantation, and convicted felon. What happened, you plugged?"

Sadly, Man reluctantly agreed. "You right, I jagged it off OG, and it's been eating away at my soul every day for the last several months. Naw, ion mess wit no gangs, especially now that I'm in here cuz of them. My rappy is plugged and got me caught up on a body saving our lives."

"So you caught a murda?"

"I was originally charged with murder, yeah, but they offered me a deal for an accessory, and I reluctantly hopped on it."

"Ah, okay. So, what'd they end up sticking you with?"

"Four wit 80% and a year good time."

"Not too bad. Enough to figure your life out, get your priorities in order, and move right. But your life, as you once knew it is dead. I'm sure you know this already. However, hope ain't lost. You just gotta venture into a different, profitable venue to accomplish your goals. And consider leaving Chicago, the economy doesn't have much to offer felons."

"Ion know if it's gonna be quite that easy, but I'll figure something out. Mind if I work out with you, OG, and relieve some of this tension?"

"Hop on in. I got a few sets left that should help you out. Don't hurt the old man tho."

Man completed Latif's workout and did a few extra sets to knock off the edge he felt since Latif's athletic reminder earlier.

Latif waited for Man to finish his extra sets and chatted Man up while trying to pinpoint the weird internal experiences he was having. He knew he didn't know Man personally, he had been locked up longer than he had been alive, however, he didn't disregard the feelings he was having.

Latif and Man walked back to their housing unit. "I get down at least three times a week with fluctuating intensities. You're welcome to join me any time you want, it'll help you stay outta trouble, especially since you're not plugged." Latif let Man know.

Diamond and her parents supported Man in every way they could throughout his prison stint. They sent him money, cards, stamps, books, and mail regularly. He rotated in calling them every couple of days and had video visits with them as often as possible, more so with his grandparents than Diamond since he didn't want them stepping into a prison to visit him. Man didn't want for anything, and he only missed canteen by choice.

Over the next several months, Man's relationships with Ball and Latif evolved. Man was relatively easy to get along with, albeit he was often introversively quiet. His relationship with Latif was more fast-paced than with Ball as Latif was older, smarter, more experienced, and into his fitness and health–a feat that was majorly important to Man. Not to mention Man's inquisitive nature and Latif's seemingly expansive wealth of knowledge. The two were destined to mesh well. While Ball was a smart thug, his life was devoted to the gang culture while Latif, several years older, had an affinity for reading almost any book he touched and keeping his former boxing skills polished. The discipline Latif had maintained over his life had somewhat mirrored the discipline Man had also exhibited in his own life.

    Man didn't have a clue of all these foreign phrases he'd heard Latif say repeatedly, and he was curious about their meanings, yet he didn't feel comfortable questioning him as a stranger, so he patiently waited for their relationship to develop to his comfort before he began asking about what he had learned was Arabic, a universal language amongst Muslims.

From his interactions with and questioning of Latif, Man learned Latif had been Muslim for 10 years, preferred to be alone rather than amongst people beyond what his current circumstances required. He earned his associate and bachelor's degrees in prison, and a paralegal diploma as well. He was serving a 40 year prison sentence at 100% for murder. Most of his family had fallen off throughout his incarceration. Latif cared deeply for the youth. He was a former winner of Chicago's Golden Gloves boxing tournament in the heavyweight division; and over the years, he gained a distinctive peace that most, even staff, envied.

Latif was a well-rounded guy and he rarely, if ever, let things get under his skin. He was, to say the least, one-of-a-kind, and Man had an affinity for Latif because he differed from the other OGs—he wasn't a hypocrite like the so-called gang leaders who preached a positive message while leading a contradictory lifestyle. Latif was truly living what he spoke and professed to believe in.

Man and Latif spent every day of six months together working out; building intellectually; avoiding the prison politics; and just shooting the breeze. He would incessantly ask Latif questions because he was young and impressionable. At this stage of his llife, all he knew was school, sports, surviving in the trenches, and Christianity somewhat according to the Southern Baptist ministry delegation.

"What made you become Islamic?" Man asked one day.

Latif laughed at the question and then explained, "Good brother, I'm Muslim--that's the proper way to say it, not Islamic. Islam is my religion, my way of life. Muslim is my identity."

"Okay. What made you become *Muslim?*" Man sarcastically asked. "Were you raised Muslim?"

"No, I wasn't raised Muslim. I converted from Christianity. Like yourself, I was a rather curious individual in search for the truth. I developed a passion for reading when I got popped. For approximately two or more years, I abandoned religion in its entirety and just prayed, asking God to lead me to His truth while continuing to read. I learned a little about different religions, and then one day, alhamdu lillah, I got my hands on a book that was used to answer my prayer and change my life forever. After I finished reading the book, I attended the next Jumu'a service with a heavily convicted heart to take shahada."

"What's all these words you're saying in a different language? What language is it and why are you speaking it?"

"Arabic. It's the language the Holy Qur'an was revealed in and is the universal language of the Muslims. No matter what country or continent you go to or what native tongue a Muslim speaks, *all* of us know what these basic terms you hear me use mean. 'Alhamdu lillah' means 'all praise to God'. 'Jumu'a' means 'Friday' in Arabic and that's the day of congregational worship incumbent upon all pubescent, sane, and resident Muslim boys and men to attend. 'Shahada' is what is commonly defined as a declaration of faith. The shahada is one of the five pillars of Islam, and it is necessary for any person wanting to become Muslim to not only profess the shahada but to also absolutely believe in what they've professed."

"So Jumu'a is like 'church' for the Muslims?"

"You can say that to a very narrow degree, but it's much different. If you're open, I can bring you to Jumu'a as my guest so you can check it out."

"Aight, bet. I'll let you know when I'm ready, but not right now. What do y'all say and believe in this declaration?"

"We say 'ash hadu an la ilaha illallah, wa ash hadu anna Muhammadan abduhu wa rasuluhu.' The English translation is 'I bear witness that there is no god but Allah, and I bear witness that Muhammad (sallallahu alayhi wa salaam) is His slave and Messenger. As Muslims, we're required to believe in this sincerely because doubting either aspect removes us from the folds of Islam."

"That's what's up. You mentioned earlier that a book led to you becoming Muslim?"

"Yes. It's titled 'Sufficient Provision For Seekers Of The Path Of Truth' by Shaykh Abdul Qadir Jilani (rahimahu Allah). It's a five-volume series, but volume two is what Allah used to remove some of the spiritual veils I carried. After reading that book, I knew the truth. I then went and sought a Holy Qur'an to confirm or disprove what I had read in volume two. By the Friday after I had completed reading the book, I had read enough of volume two and the Qur'an to be convinced of their authenticity and the direction for me, so I took shahada and never looked back. I also had my people order the five-volume set for me."

"Wow, that's dope! Why y'all be selling them pies and newspapers on the corner, and be dressed the same?"

Latif burst in laughter. "That's the 'Nation of Islam' not al-Islam or orthodox Islam. We don't consider them Muslim. That is more of a black cult, so to speak, but many of them have left the Nation, as it's known, and come to Islam alhamdu lillah. The Nation creed doesn't conciliate with any Islamic creed. For example, they believe that the black man and woman are gods and goddesses of the One true God. Muslims *only* believe in the *One* and *Only* True God—Allah. Believing in anything more than that precludes you from entering the folds of al-Islam.

Muslims don't sell 'The Final Call' newspaper nor bean pies on corners. That's a Nation thing. The Nation only exists in the US, al-Islam exists in several continents and countries. Also, the Nation, as a whole, wears suits and bow ties, you don't really see Muslims commonly dressed that way."

"Ahh, okay. That makes sense. I never knew who those dudes were, only that they were black militants like the Black Panthers or something. That book you talmbout, you still got it?"

"Yes sir. Pull up when we go in, and I'll shoot it to you," Latif replied, then resumed picking his brain about Man. Why did he look so familiar? He still couldn't put his finger on it.

21

While Man was in Centralia doing his bid and getting mental and physical exercise, L was still in the county jail, going back and forth to court appearances to prepare for trial. After six months of postponing, Kristin finally got the assistant state attorney to make a plea bargain offer to L for twenty-four years at 100%. Kristin shared the plea bargain with L during an attorney visit.

"I ain't takin' no damn twenty-four years, that fool tweakin' shordy, and you is too for bringing it back to me. They gone have to gimme that, on gang. I wouldn't get out til I'm 41, what I look like?"

"Honestly Lamont, I'm on the fence with this deal. I think it's a good and bad offer. You murdered a man in cold blood and there's no evidence contrary thereto. Sure, Mr. McCarren had a pistol on him, but there's no video footage or eyewitnesses that reveal you knew he had the pistol, let alone that he displayed it with the intent or willingness to use it. So, for that reason, I think 24 years is a reasonable deal under the circumstances. The decedent's gun was on the floor near his body, rather than on his person, and he also has a record for perpetrating acts of violence against various victims. As a 17-year-old kid I think you may have been petrified for your life in that store. Not to mention the number of murders that have occurred in urban Chicago stores in recent years. And for those reasons, I think it's a poor offer by the state. However, by law, I'm required to present the offer to you because ultimately, you're the decision-maker of your fate. Give me some more time to soften him up and see if he'll come down. What is your bottom line in terms of a deal?"

"No more than 15 years at 85%, straight up, and *that's pushing it*. Kristin, that stud was coming in there to kill us, period. I know y'all prolly can't understand this in y'all suburban world, but in da trenches this what we know, what we do – it's kill or be killed, and I did what I had to to protect me and my rappy. If I didn't kill dat mark, CPD woulda been zippin' up two body bags instead of one, on fo nem."

"Lamont, I understand the sociological effects of our urban communities. I may have been blessed to not grow up in the hood, but I certainly didn't grow up with a silver spoon in my mouth, either. I've had and currently have friends from the hood, so I certainly understand the struggles our people face in their respective environments. Not to mention I've seen and represented several Chicago clients like yourself that have essentially become a product of their environment for survival. I get it, although I may not like or agree with it. I get it, I really do, but it's these prosecutors that must be convinced, so let me see what other offers I can get you."

"That's what my brother paid you for. You supposed to be da *best* in da City, *that's why* we hired you to get me da *best* scenario in dis flukey ass case. They ain't got *nothing* on me 'cept dat video, and it don't even got audio to tell da whole story, you *know* it. Mr. Jed said he didn't catch what transpired cuz he was talkin' to us while watchin' TV behind da counter. My rappy ain't said nothin'. I ain't said nothin, and da video shows dis fool, grown ass man, come in da sto tryna punk us and he was strapped! I ain't tryna go to da box and pick *nothin'*. Get me a sweet deal so I can get on wit my life!"

"Lamont, your point is well taken. Now let me get something clear with you so that we can agree from this point forward, otherwise, I will advise your brother there's been a breakdown in the attorney-client relationship and I'll happily return unspent funds and withdraw my representation of you so that you all can hire an attorney that you can talk to as you please.

"Foremost, I am *not* one of those little girls you're probably used to dealing with. I am a grown woman, and you *will* respect me as such, or my representation will end immediately. Second, I am not some shabby ass lawyer like some, if not most, of my colleagues. I take my job *seriously*, and I fight my best for *each* of my clients, and that's exactly why I have the success and reputation that I do. I understand you're frustrated with your situation and find the State's offer offensive, understandably so. However, I brought you this offer because I'm legally required to, not because I'm co-signing it. There will probably be one or two more offers and when I feel that I've gotten you the best offer I can, you'll know. I don't need *you* to tell me how to do my job, I'm 15-1 on murder trials alone, and you have yet to experience a trial, so you must trust me through this process and know that I'm going to do the best I can. Are we on the same team or not?"

"We good."

"Good, let's keep it that way and I'll see you in 2-3 weeks, hopefully with a new offer. I have my investigator talking to the store owner, Michael Jed, and tracking down any potential witnesses that I can use as leverage with the prosecutor. Take care of yourself and get in school while you're in here if you already haven't.

<u>Saturday, March 23, 2024</u>

It was a decent morning in the Centralia prison yard. Latif and Man were at the beginning of their workout and having their regular stimulating conversation throughout their workout. Man, directed the conversation with his curiosity by talking about the book he picked up from Latif–Sufficient Provision For Seekers Of The Path Of Truth.

"I don't understand all I've read in that book so far, but I'm doing my best to digest everything I'm reading. The Arabic terms and Muslim practices are foreign to me, but overall, I'm enjoying the book. No cap, I be in it heavy, day and night, I even started taking notes cuz it's interesting, and I believe beneficial, things I was unaware of in there that I don't wanna forget. Things I ain't never heard of. It's crazy too cuz outside of school and sports, dis the first book I ever read cover-to-cover."

"You're not gonna understand everything you read, especially on the first go-round. That's an excellent practice to take notes when you read. Your notes can serve as good refreshers because your mind isn't gonna recall everything you read, say, a week from now. Tell you what, since you're reading it like you are and enjoying it, that's my gift to you. Keep the book."

In complete awe, Man looked at Latif with widened eyes. "Fa real?" he asked excitedly.

"Yes, it belongs to you now. I already made my intentions to give it to you as sadaqa, I can order another."

"Naw, I can't take your book, then your collection will be messed up cuz you gave me volume two of five."

"It's too late, good brother, I've already made my intentions to give it to you. As a Muslim, I can't accept it back. Enjoy it, I'll get another."

"Wow. Thanks, Latif. I truly appreciate it. It's the only gift I've gotten in jail. I didn't know they give gifts in prison. I would've thought y'all was too hard for that kinda stuff. I plan to read it several times until I'm satisfied with my understanding of it, which means I'll prolly be asking you a ton of questions if you don't mind."

"No problem, Man. I'm at your service."

"Latif, can I ask you a personal question?"

"Sure."

"OG, I been with you all these months day in and day out. I've seen how you move with your Muslim brothers and everyone else, including me, and honestly, I can't see how you could wind up in prison with all this time with *your* personality. What happened with you? How you catch a body as chill as you are?"

Latif took a deep breath to get rid of the sudden pressure that gripped his chest and the frog that was squeezing his throat tightly. "Man, in nineteen years I've never had this conversation with anyone that wasn't a lawyer representing me. This isn't the first time I've been asked that same question, and honestly, I put the case long behind me after losing the trial, vowing to take it to my grave. The crime happened before I took shahada so it's truly nobody's business, per Islamic protocol, but I'll share it with you, young blood. Just please keep my business to yourself for me as a solid."

"My word, you got that. But if it's gonna violate your Islamic beliefs or make you uncomfortable, don't worry about it. It's good."

"It's okay. I consider you to be my little buddy. I don't mind telling you my truth. Before I tell you my story, let me tell you this: never judge by a person's face, demeanor, or personality to determine if they'd kill. Even a loving mother who's never harmed a soul would kill given the right circumstances. I understand where you're coming from, as I once thought the same way. Over the years, though, I've learned that sometimes it's the ones you least expect to be killers that have more bodies than a prostitute, especially in Chicago--shordies learn to kill nowadays before they learn to fight."

"Straight up, that's real." I didn't expect my rappy to be as cold as he is. We been best friends since we was 9 in da Jackie Robinson league and I ain't never seen or heard of that side of him. So, I get it."

"When I was out there, hard times came and I was on my ass, ya dig. My ol' lady and I was living together, both of us working, but after the bills was paid, I'd have nearly nothing left in my pocket. We was making do, but I was tired of struggling, living check-to-check. It seemed no matter what I did, I could never get ahead. It was always just surviving. I knew nothing about investing or where to even begin. Hell, I didn't even know nobody that was investing unless it was drugs or something. That wasn't an option for me. I'm not the criminal type. None of it appealed to me. I didn't want to end up *here*.

"I tried the Chicago boxing league and excelled at it. I even won the Golden Gloves tournament back in the day, but that didn't go anywhere either. Anyway, I had a buddy who told me he could put $50k cash in my pocket if I helped him with a 'play'. When I asked for more details, turns out he knew a well-known drug dealer seeking to get rid of his competition so the City would be his. He assured me it was an easy play and that he'd already investigated everything, but he didn't want to do it by himself because it was not that simple; and second, in case it went bad, his family would know the truth. The plug had $100k for his competitor's head. We'd split it 50/50 and get half up front and the other half after the murder."

Man's jaws dropped. "Damn Latif! Don't tell me you killed for money. Why not just sell drugs or rob? At least you would've been out by now if you got popped."

Latif looked at Man in his eyes and said, "I used to ask myself that same question often."

Man had a very distinct and attentive look in his eyes that pierced Latif's brain faster than the speed of light, and in that very moment, his chest compressed heavily. At first, Latif thought he was having a heart attack, and then his mind time-warped to nineteen years ago. He saw himself in his mind, roughly twenty years younger, and he was wearing the *exact* outfit that he knew he burned after committing his crime.

A tear uncontrollably rolled down his cheek. He was confused by what was happening. Man took a step towards him because Latif was non-responsive. It all came pouring down on him like a Canadian avalanche. It was making sense now. Latif took a step back from Man. Briefly, he had lost his inability to speak, think, or even function. He felt like his total being had been captured. Slowly, his senses returned, and he could only utter in a trembling voice, "Man… Man, I'm sorry young brother." He continued stumbling backward.

"What? Are you okay, Latif? What you talmbout? Sorry for what?"

"Man, I wasn't supposed to be the shooter. My rappy froze up with the gun, my victim saw both of our faces—he *had* to die, that's what we came for. If he didn't die, we both would've been dead within 24 hours. I raised my pistol, put it to his head, and squeezed the trigger twice. The look he had in his eyes before I killed him was the same image I just saw in your eyes. I'll never forget it. You're a spitting image of him, just a younger version without a beard."

Man laughed and responded, "M*annn*, you tweakin' Joe. My daddy died from cancer years ago." Then he thought about how long ago his father passed away and then he did the math. "Hell naw!" Man was slightly concerned now, but still did not believe Latif.

"What … what's your mother's name, Man?" Latif stuttered, still in shock.

"What?! Why?"

"Please, tell me your mother's name."

"Diamond Williams." Man's frustration and anger were clear in his answer and his facial expressions.

"Yaa Allah!" More tears ran down Latif's face.

That was all Man needed to see to be convinced. He was overcome with anger. His mother had lied to him his whole life and her lie was now exposed by some random stranger that he's gotten cool with. He wanted to attack Latif, but he knew he didn't stand a chance, given his strength and boxing background.

Man turned and walked away angrily. He went back to his housing unit and called Diamond's cellphone twice. Diamond didn't answer her phone because she was at work. Man hung up and dialed Carrie's number. His call was answered and accepted without delay. He tried to keep calm despite his chest pumping hard, like he'd just walked off the field for a break in a football game. "Hey grandma, how are you?"

"I'm fine baby. How are you?"

"I'm not too good, grandma. Can you text my mom and tell her I said to get up here ASAP? I tried calling her, but she's not answering."

"Of course I can. I'll do it right now. What's wrong? Is everything okay, Man?"

"I'm good grandma, I just have a bone to pick with my mom, that's all. So please emphasize to her my position. I'm not gonna call her again until I talk to her in person. I gotta go grandma, I love you."

"Okay sweetheart, I understand, and I'll convey your message. Call me back when you cool down, okay? I love you too, Man, and you be careful in there. Bye-bye."

Man got off the phone and retrieved his shower stuff from his cell where he unexpectedly ran into Ball inside their cell. Man's voice cracked "What's up, bro?"

"What's da deal Gang, what you on?"

"Coolin, bouta hop in da shower. Aye, check it out, bro. I know y'all protocol, bro, but on da low can you slide me a piece?"

Ball looked at Man. "You fa real folks."

"Yeah, I gotta stand on some bidness."

Ball closed the door so they could talk privately. "What's up Gang, is it *that* serious you gotta book somebody and risk jaggin off yo date?"

"I just found out it's a stud on the yard that's in here fo killin my daddy. I'm not inclined to let it go."

"Whoa! Dat's heavy, G. You gotta do whatchu gotta do, bro, straight up. Dis a once in a lifetime opportunity to get yo man. Who he under?"

"He not under y'all, that's all you need to know. When can you get dat to me?"

"Check it out. Gone get yo shower, sleep on what you feelin' right now, and if you still feelin' da same tomorrow, I gotchu, on da guys. Right now, you thinkin' outta anger G, I'm not gone let you go out like dat."

22

<u>Sunday, March 24, 2024</u>

"Inmate Williams, cell 128. You have a visit," said a feminine voice over the prison's public announcement system. A couple of minutes later, a pass was slid through the door crack. "Williams, you ready?"

"Yeah," Man answered as he finished getting dressed.

The cell door opened a few seconds later and as Man was exiting the cell Ball said "Have a good one, bro."

"Good lookin', Ball."

Man walked to the visiting room and saw Diamond sitting in a chair at a table by herself with her head down looking completely broken emotionally. When he reached the table, Diamond looked Man in his eyes and saw the anger and disappointment present that she'd never seen in her son before now. That look confirmed what she suspected, Man somehow found out about Note. He pulled out the chair and sat down. Silence loomed over them briefly before Man broke it. "How long was you planning to keep your lie going?!"

"What lie, Man?" Diamond said softly as she halfway balled up the tissue in her hand.

"Don't sit up here and play crazy with me. You know *damn* well what I'm talking about. My father!"

Diamond used the folded tissue to dab the corner of her eyes as the tears began flowing, one after another. She removed the brown, permed hair from over her eye and looked up at Man once again. "Son, I'm sorry."

"I don't wanna hear dat sorry crap right now, answer my question," he demanded in an elevated voice.

"I planned to sit you down after you graduated and tell you everything."

"Yeah, well that plan was derailed cuz I found out from some stranger in here that I got cool wit that he's in here for killin' my daddy. And according to him, he knows I'm my daddy son cuz I'm a 'spitting image' of him, only I don't have a beard. Now I'm here battling confusing emotions and debating if I should get my lick back and kill him just as he killed my daddy. I wanna deprive his family of the same things he deprived me and you of for $50k."

Diamond's tears poured profusely. She dropped her head a third time to use her hair to hide her reddened face and tears from everyone surrounding her and Man in the visiting room. "Baby, you're my only child, and I've sacrificed my life for you. Please, don't throw your life away."

"Tell me everything. There's nothing else for us to discuss on dis visit. I wanna know everything up until he was murdered."

"Okay," Diamond sniffled. She patted her eyes and gently blew all of the buildup snot lingering in her nose. She took a deep breath and exhaled. "I met your father after I graduated from Julian and was coming out of the CSU registration office like I told you. I told you his birth name, but he was known as 'Note' to everyone. His mother was a retired prostitute of his father, who was a well-known pimp. Your grandfather was killed by one of his prostitutes in a rage of some sort that wasn't made clear to me. He had life insurance on him and his wife, plus he had a decent amount of money saved up from his profession. Your grandmother gave the savings to Note and split the life insurance payout with him so that he could have a decent life. Note used that money to invest in multiple businesses and his drug empire that began after opening his first business. He ultimately became the biggest drug dealer in Chicago. He owned this City.

"Note and I were together about six months when I got pregnant with you. Before getting pregnant, he would use me for tasks like picking up money from designated locations or traveling a couple cars behind him as a trail car when it was necessary for him to use the e-way so I could be an additional set of eyes. When I found out I was pregnant, I was both devastated and happy. I could no longer take the risks I was taking. I told Note I was pregnant and tried talking to him about us being a family; him leaving the game, and us living the right way. He was completely unhappy and was refusing to accept any of it. While he was okay with me not running for or with him, he completely rejected the idea of being a father, having a family, or being a husband.

"After a while, he realized I was gonna see my pregnancy through and there was nothing he could do or say to me to convince me otherwise. He stuck around for a couple of months, probably thinking I'd cave into an abortion. By the end of my first trimester, he told me straight up that his future and mine didn't align. I went off on him because I realized that you'd probably grow up without a father, without *your* father. He had his bodyguard escort me out of his business.

"A few days later he contacted me and had me come to the warehouse to have further talk. When I arrived, he took me into his office where there was a travel bag on his desk that had $250k cash in it. He handed me the bag and told me he was sorry he couldn't go any further with me and that the money was more than enough for me to invest and take care of you and me for the rest of our lives if I invested properly. He also gave me his personal broker's card to assist me with investing. I took the card and bag of money, then spat in his face and told him he'd regret his decision. Again, I was escorted to my car by his bodyguard.

"Two weeks after I last spoke to or saw your father, he was murdered at the warehouse. The morning after his murder, I was leaving my parents' house to go to a follow-up doctor's appointment for my pregnancy. As soon as I got into my car and closed the door, I heard a tap on the window that startled me. It was J-Boogie, Note's bodyguard, pointing a pistol at me with his finger on the trigger, telling me to unlock my car doors. When I hit the unlock button, he got in the backseat behind me and put his pistol to my left side between the driver's side door and the driver's seat. I was unaware there was another goon with a pistol on my passenger side with a pistol also until he got in my car and pointed his pistol at me so nobody could see it. J-Boogie asked me where was the money Note gave me. At first I thought they were robbing me, but after I gave the money to them and they saw wasn't a dollar missing, they revealed to me why they came.

"'Note was killed last night. I know you had something to do with it, and as soon as I get the confirmation, you and this baby will be joining Note' J-Boogie told me. Note's goons left and I collapsed on the floor and sobbed like never before. Everything had just crumbled in on me, and now I was also scared to death for my life. I knew J-Boogie wasn't leaving me with an empty threat, Note's crew didn't play, this was well-known, and that's probably why they suspected me. As quick as they left, I took three thousand out of that money and bought my pistol, extra clips and *plenty* of bullets the same day. I carried that pistol daily and everywhere for two months until this guy was arrested for Note's murder.

"When the word got out there was an arrest for Note's murder, J-Boogie got on it instantly. Rumor had it that J-Boogie linked up with Note's plug in CPD and got everything he could on him. J-Boogie put a bag on the guy's head on two separate occasions to have him killed, but it only resulted in him being stabbed both times. It was said J-Boogie was at that guy's trial daily to hear the evidence and see if he actually committed the murder and to see if I had any involvement with it. They were out for blood. It wasn't until after the trial was over, I got another visit from J-Boogie to apologize to me for all that he'd put me through, and he told me they were now 100% certain I had nothing to do with Note's murder.

"I stayed away from the trial and Note's goons and family to the best of my ability for these reasons."

Man took in all of this information and sat speechless. More confusion had descended upon him. His anger diminished towards his mother slightly, but now he wanted to kill the goons that tormented his mother as well as kill Latif. "What's up wit dem studs that was tweakin wit you Ma, dey still alive?"

"Son, please, you aren't a killer. Forget about them and this guy in prison. Come home. You have a future ahead of you after this journey. I raised you differently. Kill people with your success, not anger."

Man sat quietly for a few minutes pondering over everything, then he felt the urge to apologize to Diamond for his behavior towards her.
"Mama, this is a lot to process, but I need to start. Go home. I'll call you after I sort through everything. I love you." He kissed her on the cheek and then left the visiting room.

Upon entering the housing unit, Man saw Ball and pushed up on him "What's good bro?"

Ball shook Man's hand and replied, "Jus coolin, folks. You had a good one?"

"Yeah. Aye, lemme get dat piece bro," Man whispered in Ball's ear and kept pushing to their cell.

Man went inside the cell and laid back on his bunk, staring at the ceiling combing through all of his thoughts as he planned his next move ....

Part 2 Coming Soon…

Made in the USA
Middletown, DE
17 August 2024

59293983R00129